POINT OF NO RETURN

Mention the name 'Jack Bannon' and most folk would immediately say 'Bounty Hunter'. But they'd be wrong. Sure he had hunted men for money, but there had been a damn good reason for it. Like the time the mysterious woman with a dozen different names hired his gun for dollars. It was the closest he'd ever come to having his head blown off. Bannon swore that if he got out of this one alive he'd never be a bounty hunter again. If . . .

JAKE DOUGLAS

POINT OF NO RETURN

Complete and Unabridged

LINFORD
Leicester

First published in Great Britain in 1999 by
Robert Hale Limited
London

First Linford Edition
published 2000
by arrangement with
Robert Hale Limited
London

British Library CIP Data

Douglas, Jake
    Point of no return.—Large print ed.—
    Linford western library
    1. Western stories
    2. Large type books
    I. Title
    823.9'14 [F]

    ISBN 0–7089–5715–3

Published by
F. A. Thorpe (Publishing)
Anstey, Leicestershire

Set by Words & Graphics Ltd.
Anstey, Leicestershire
Printed and bound in Great Britain by
T. J. International Ltd., Padstow, Cornwall

1

Caught!

Jack Bannon pushed through the bat-wings of the Santa Fe saloon, stepped slowly outside, paused to roll and light a cigarette as he squinted against the bright sunlight.

Even with his wide shoulders pushed against the adobe wall in a half-slouch while he went through the simple, automatic motions, he looked tall. Standing straight he would top the six-four mark without his hat or high-heeled riding boots. At the ends of long arms he had thick wrists which bespoke strength in those long-fingered hands deftly manipulating paper and tobacco flakes. His square jaw was stubbled, his hair long and untidy where it overhung the worn collar of his shirt. The vest had seen better days and the denim trousers were faded and trail-stained. Only the six-gun in the holster worn on his right thigh showed signs of having received recent attention, gleaming dully with a patina of oil that was free of dust and grit.

He raised the cigarette towards his wide mouth, tongue running along the edge of the paper in the shadow of his bent nose: it had obviously seen some rough times in the past. There were a few other small scars on the hawkish face: a couple over each eyebrow, one on the right cheek, another on the right side of his jaw. The eyes were blue and clear enough despite the long gruelling trails behind him.

They searched idly around the plaza now as he dragged on the cigarette, deeply and satisfyingly. The sweeping gaze stopped, narrowed sharply.

Suddenly his shoulders were thrusting him off the wall. The cigarette was flung, mangled, into the gutter and he was moving forward with long, purposeful strides. His speed increased when he stepped down to the plaza and started across, caring nothing for the traffic. It is doubtful that he even heard the curses of the man who had to haul up his buckboard team with a savage wrench of the reins. A rider swore as he dodged his mount around Bannon but he kept on, eyes fixed on something — or someone — on the far side of the plaza.

It was a horseman. A man in a short buckskin jacket and a high-crowned hat, forking a decent-looking bay gelding, shouldering pedestrians aside so he could reach the water trough under the cottonwood on the north side of the plaza.

He was walking the mount in, the bay's head already lowering towards the water, when Bannon strode up and, without a word, reached for the rider's belt and heaved. The man was so startled he didn't let go the reins and the bay whinnied as its head was jerked around and it stumbled. But by that time, its rider was flying through the air and, as the horse righted itself with an angry snort, the man hit the dust with a grunt.

Bannon was still holding onto the belt, yanked upright, the leather biting into the other ranny's midriff. He gagged and Bannon kicked him in the side three times, hard and fast, before letting go. The man drew up his legs and rolled in the dust, grunting and moaning in pain.

Through squinted eyes, he looked up at Bannon who had the sun behind him, but then the man moved slightly and he was able to see his face.

The downed man's eyes widened and his face looked kind of pale as he swore and started to scramble to his feet.

Bannon kicked him again and he rolled almost to the feet of the men in the front row of the crowd that was gathering.

'Let him get up!' someone growled.

Bannon looked down at the grimacing man. 'Someone wants me to play fair with you, Birch — that the way you play it? That what you did with Cap Burrows . . . ?'

Bannon stepped in as Birch climbed slowly to his feet, clipped the man on the side of the jaw, sank a fist into his midriff and dropped him to his knees with another cracking blow to the jaw. He swayed there, blood dribbling from his mouth. Bannon lifted a knee into his face and the nose went with a wet crunchy sound. Men shouted from the crowd, but when Bannon looked up, two who had been about to intervene suddenly stepped back and wouldn't meet his gaze.

But Birch made use of the brief diversion.

He launched himself at Bannon, wrapped his arms about his legs and brought him down into the dust where they rolled and scrabbled for position. Birch managed to drop a knee into Bannon's belly and then climb on top. He sledged several hard blows into the man's face and Bannon grunted, felt flesh tear and a little blood flow. He

5

caught the next fist in his hand and twisted savagely, taking Birch unawares. The man yelled as he lost balance and spilled sideways into the dust. Bannon kicked out from under and they both scrambled upright.

For a moment they stood facing each other, fists clenched, bloody, sweaty, caked with dust and blood. Then as of one accord they ran at each other and the thud as they hit sounded like a wild mustang driving himself against a corral fence. They staggered back and then started swinging. Fists hit with meat-cleaver sounds and heads snapped back. Bannon's hat flew off to one side — Birch had lost his earlier, revealing his bald pate which now was bleeding from a small wound.

Bannon lifted an already sore and bruised forearm, blocking a blow, ducking in underneath. He slammed a fist into Birch's chest, but the man was moving back and the blow lacked power. Bannon swiftly stepped after him, using both fists now, arms working like pistons as he kept Birch on the retreat, the man vainly trying to block the hammering blows. He stumbled, gasping for breath, then lowered his head and butted Bannon in the chest, snapped his head up so that the top of his skull connected with Bannon's jaw.

The man stumbled away, putting down a hand to keep from falling all the way into the dust. Birch leapt in, kicking, trying to rake him open with his spur rowels. Bannon rolled but felt the bite of a spiked rowel across his left bicep. It snagged in the shirt material briefly, and Birch fought to keep balance on one leg.

Bannon grabbed the other, heaved, and Birch went down but scrambled swiftly away on all fours. As he staggered up, in front of a Mexican flower stall under a sapling awning, Bannon launched himself bodily at the man. The Mexican woman screamed and threw up her arms as she hurriedly dodged the two crashing bodies. The frail bench collapsed under their weight and the gaudy blossoms were crushed, releasing various sweet odours to mix with those of sweat and smoky trails and blood and splintered wood.

Birch kicked wildly and one boot caught Bannon alongside the head. He floundered and Birch snatched up a broken length of sapling, came roaring, and swung a murderous blow at Bannon's head. Bannon dropped flat and the club smashed into the earth inches in front of his face. He snatched at it with both hands, got a grip and tore it from Birch's clawing fingers. The man spun away and then came spinning back, palming up his six-gun.

Bannon hurled the club at him, rolling, wrenched around onto his belly, elbow driving hard against the ground for support as his Colt bucked against his wrist.

The crash of Birch's gun was lost in the hammering roar of Bannon's weapon and the man staggered, tried to keep balance, was smashed back by the second bullet into the adobe wall. The third one drove him sideways and he spilled awkwardly over a pail of flowers that had escaped the earlier demolition, rolled off and flopped onto his back, glazing eyes staring up at the hot Santa Fe sky through the collapsed sapling roof. He tried to push upright, fell onto his side . . . The plaza had gone very quiet. The echoes of the gunfire seemed to fade slowly, diminishing as they rolled away amongst the adobe buildings.

The crowd stared, some looking down at the dead man, others watching Jack Bannon swiftly replace the used shells in his smoking Colt.

There was a young blonde woman in a pretty dark-green and white frock standing on the walk outside a dress shop who seemed to pay him more attention than was warranted for a lady of her looks and elegance. Bannon's glance, roving the crowd, paused, looked her over, while he reloaded by expert touch alone. He moved his gaze on — in case Birch had friends who might want to square things.

But no one made any hostile moves, though the Mexican flower woman clawed at his arm, speaking rapid and angry Spanish, plainly wanting compensation for her crushed flowers. Almost absently, Bannon pulled a couple of coins from his pocket and pushed them into the brown clawed hand. The woman glanced down and suddenly her words stopped, her eyes widened and her jaw dropped. Then she bowed several times, repeating '*Gracias, señor, muchas gracias!*' and backed away.

Bannon was still giving his attention to the crowd, but they mostly stood around, staring at Birch's body.

Except the man who came running up holding a long-barrelled Greener shotgun, the hard sunlight reflecting from the brass star dragging at his shirt pocket.

'All right, mister, just drop that gun! And I mean now!'

Bannon snapped his head up as the shotgun's hammers cocked. He closed the loading gate, spun the cylinder and dropped the gun — back into his holster.

The sheriff — a bulky man who looked fit despite the paunch of middle-age — narrowed his eyes.

'I said drop it!'

'It's safe where it is, Sheriff,' Bannon told him, hooking his thumbs into his gunbelt. He blinked some blood out of his left eye, swayed a little, battered and weary but totally unafraid.

The sheriff frowned. 'You just kill that man?' The twin barrels jerked an inch in Birch's direction.

Bannon nodded. 'Fair fight — ask anyone.'

'Fair enough when it come down to guns, Sheriff,' a townsman spoke up, looking tight-lipped at Bannon. 'But looked like they hated each other's guts, the way this ranny hauled the other out of the saddle and started right in to kick his spine loose.'

Others backed the speaker and the sheriff turned hard eyes to Bannon. He looked him over, top to toe, and seemed a little more wary now. 'That right? You started it? You and this feller know each other?'

'I've been following him for six months and nigh on a thousand miles, Sheriff. He was Birch Brazos.'

'Who you say . . . ?'

Bannon didn't repeat the name: it was clear the lawman knew Brazos' moniker, but was startled to think the man had been in his town.

'And who the hell might you be?'

'Jack Bannon.' That was enough by way of explanation, he figured.

And he saw by the lawman's face that it was. Very slowly, the sheriff used his boot toe to push Brazos over onto his back, bent a little from the waist to stare down into the wide-eyed bloody features. He grunted, straightened slowly and looked bleakly at Jack Bannon.

'And the bounty on Brazos' head had

nothing to do with your jumping him in my town and shooting him down?'

'Maybe it didn't have as much to do with it as you think, Sheriff,' Bannon said mildly, using his neckerchief now to mop his face. Someone had given him back his battered hat and he jammed it carelessly on his head.

'But the dodger said 'dead or alive', huh?'

Bannon shrugged. 'I didn't go for my gun first.'

'Saying it was his choice — well, why not? If he figured you were gonna take him alive all he had to look forward to was a hangman's noose. You better come with me. And keep your hands away from that six-shooter.' The lawman turned to the crowd. 'Merry, Tab, get a door from somewhere and take Brazos down to the undertaker. Tell him not to do anything to him till I've taken another look.'

The two men indicated moved away, grumbling, and Bannon started to walk across the plaza in the direction indicated by the sheriff's shotgun.

He didn't notice the young blonde woman in the green and white dress watching him closely. Then a train whistle bleated down at the depot and she threw a rather startled look in that direction, hurried away without another glance at Bannon.

In the law office, the sheriff introduced himself as Miles Baker, told Bannon to take a seat, but he stood himself, seeming to be more at ease when he was standing over the other.

'Bounty hunters ain't welcome in my town, Bannon.'

'Find that a lot, now you mention it, Sheriff.'

'Stow that sarcasm! I got no time for you killers.'

'Speaking personally, Sheriff, I don't kill all the men I hunt down.'

'Just the ones whose guts you hate, huh?'

Bannon said nothing, reached for his tobacco and papers, seeing the lawman tense.

'What have you personally against Birch Brazos?'

Bannon made the cigarette, taking his time, and lit up, blowing a cloud of smoke before answering. 'He was a real mean bastard.'

Miles Baker waited for elaboration but Bannon just smoked silently.

'You claiming the reward?'

'Why not? The price was on his head and I'm the one who killed him.'

'I don't like you, Bannon. Never have.'

Bannon frowned. 'We've never met before.'

'Didn't have to — I just don't like bounty hunters. And I didn't like specially what I heard about you.' If the sheriff was expecting Bannon to ask just what he'd heard, he was disappointed: the bounty hunter simply continued to smoke casually. 'Go after a man and don't give up no matter what — killing folk who get in your way — just so's you can get your blood

15

money! You're no better'n the men you hunt down!'

Bannon sighed. 'Yeah, seems to be the general opinion of bounty hunters, all right. You want to get the paperwork started now?'

Miles Baker scowled. 'What I'd like to do is kick your butt outa my town, right now!'

'You can do that after we get the paperwork out of the way, if you like.'

'Damn your sass, Bannon! You watch it or I'll have you behind bars so quick you'll think I'm a Chinee magician.'

Bannon smiled thinly. 'Not quite right about the eyes, Sheriff.'

Baker growled, went behind his desk, yanked out his chair and dropped into it. He did everything with angry, savage movements; opening a desk drawer, rummaging in it for the right claim form; slamming it shut; wrenching open another and searching for a pencil; muttering under his breath. He glared at Bannon.

'Let's get it done, damn you. Full name . . . ?'

It went slowly because the sheriff was in such a rage — and frustrated — that he either kept snapping the point of his pencil or made mistakes and had to screw up the form and start another.

They were almost through when the office doorway darkened and two men pushed inside. They brought the smell of wild trails with them and had the look of men who lived mostly in the outdoors. They glared first at Bannon and then at the sheriff.

'Wait outside,' Baker told them before they could speak. 'I'm busy now.'

The tall one with the jet-black *pistolero* moustache said, 'Busy fixin' up this ranny's claim for a bounty, Sheriff?'

Baker frowned and Bannon tensed. 'What d'you know about it?'

The man pointed a calloused finger at Bannon. 'I know he claims the man he killed was Birch Brazos, but we're

17

here to tell you his name was Joshua Lord, and he's a trail-driver, not an outlaw!'

'The hell you say!' Baker came half out of his chair, switching his gaze swiftly between the two newcomers and the seated Bannon, who sat very still and sober now.

'The hell we do, Sheriff!' growled the shorter man, a pink-skinned *hombre* with a peeling nose and thick, blistered lips. 'We been ridin' with Josh for weeks. Pushin' Jingle-Bob McCall's cows up from Amarillo. We heard about this Birch Brazos pullin' a stage hold-up over to Gallup on the San Jose and it just couldn'ta been Josh 'cause he was ridin' with us through the San Andreas Mountains, pushin' Jingle-Bob's steers. Most of the trail hands've gone back to Texas by now, but there's a couple left who'll swear to that.'

Baker was staring hard at Bannon. 'Now what you got to say about that, Bannon?'

Jack Bannon sighed. 'That wasn't Brazos who pulled that Gallup robbery; I know — I was close behind him when that happened and the trail led me down to Texas and up the Sacramento Trail to here. It's not uncommon for a wanted man to be blamed for all kinds of jobs he never pulled. Others cash in on it, fake it up so the wanted man's blamed . . . but that feller I killed was Birch Brazos, all right. You go check him out, Sheriff. He'll match the description on the dodger.'

'Well, I aimed to look him over before I put in your claim, but now I reckon you better come along and we'll all do this together . . . ' His gaze included the two cowboys who introduced themselves as Pete O'Brien and Rusty Burke. They glared at Bannon.

'Be a pleasure, Sheriff,' said O'Brien, the one with the moustache. 'Josh was a good trail pard . . . '

Bannon snorted and heaved to his feet.

Dancey watched the woman in the green and white dress at the ticket window of the railroad depot. He stayed back behind stacked freight where he could not be seen, but where he could watch as she bought her ticket.

After she walked away and down the cinders towards the stationary train, the loco panting now and getting up steam, he hurried down to the ticket window, one hand digging into his pocket. She climbed on board as he reached the window.

The ticket seller was a grey-haired man with rheumy eyes and barely glanced up. 'Where to?'

'Same place as the young woman who was just here.'

The old man glanced up in what was probably, for him, a quick movement. You could almost hear his wrinkled neck creak. 'What was that?'

Dancey slid a five-dollar piece under the window cage. 'You really deef, or did you catch me the first time?'

The old man stared at the coin, then a fluttery hand reached for it and scooped it expertly into the pocket of the drab apron he wore.

'You're wantin' to go to Albuquerque, mister?'

Dancey smiled, his thin lips pulling back tightly from tobacco-stained teeth. 'So, it's to be south again? Yeah, old-timer, Albuquerque'll do me . . . She give a name?'

The old man tore off the ticket and punched it, but said nothing, until Dancey pushed another coin under the grille. It disappeared as swiftly as the first. To the same place.

'She had her ticket booked for some time — Miss Jane Boyd. From Canyon City, Colorada — that's for free.'

Dancey smiled, took his ticket as the loco whistle shrieked and he started to run. The train was beginning to move, but he had plenty of time and swung aboard on the last car ahead of the caboose as the guard glared at him.

Dancey grinned: now he couldn't miss. It was a long way to Albuquerque and all he'd have to do was find her compartment or crowd into a seat beside her and . . .

He hurried through doors to the next car. The old train was really moving now, the car rocking, as he confidently strode down the aisle, looking for her amongst the passengers. He found her in the next car forward, sitting up front, the green dress trailing into the aisle a little. The seat beside her was vacant as he came up on her from behind. He stepped in front and sat down beside her, doffing his hat.

'Well, *Miss Jane Boyd*, you won't mind my company for a spell, I hope . . . ?'

Then his jaw fell and his stomach lurched as cold green eyes met his and a stranger's face hardened as the woman snapped, 'Sir, you have the wrong person and if you speak one more word to me, I'll call the conductor!'

Dancey was incapable of speaking. He simply stared at the strange woman, muttered a lone 'But . . . ' then lunged for the window, poked his head out and looked back at the dwindling railroad depot as the train lurched and swayed at high speed across the flats before the drop down into the valley.

He was just able to make out a small moving dot of green and white, walking away from the depot, back into Santa Fe.

He swore bitterly and turned around angrily, intending to question this woman.

'How much she pay you to act as decoy?' he demanded between clenched teeth.

The woman moved her hands out of her lap now, revealing the pearl-handled derringer, her thumb confidently cocking back the knurled hammer.

'Enough. Now you want to find somewhere else to sit? Or maybe I could scream — I notice several burly gentlemen in the car who would surely come rushing to my aid — or, I suppose this gun could *accidentally* discharge as you made to paw me?'

He reared back. 'Take it easy . . . '

'Go look for another seat, mister — in another car. This train doesn't stop until it gets to Albuquerque, but I don't want to see your ugly face again, understand?'

'Bitch!' he hissed, as he stepped past her into the aisle and made for the door leading to the car behind.

The blonde woman laughed lightly, but did not put the derringer away.

2

'Get Out!'

Bannon casually knocked the sheriff's hand aside and pointed to the fresh wound on Birch Brazos' left cheek.

'There's scar tissue under that. Guess my knuckles split it open during the fight.'

Miles Baker was holding a wanted dodger that listed the identifying marks to be found on Birch Brazos. He looked up with bleak eyes and the beginning of a crooked smile.

'I don't see no scar there.' He turned to O'Brien and Burke. 'You boys . . . ?'

They didn't even bother looking, held cold gazes on Bannon.

'We don't see nothin' that matches what you got on that dodger, Sheriff,' said O'Brien. 'Tell you, it ain't Brazos.'

Jack Bannon looked at the trio. 'So

that's the way you're gonna play it . . . you, Baker, because you just naturally don't like bounty hunters, specially in your town; and you two — because Brazos was a pard of yours and you don't aim to see me collect the bounty for nailing him.'

The trail men scowled but Baker stayed calm.

'Well, we ain't found anything yet to match up. Oh, I give you the height and colouring is close enough, but this ranny's a deal skinnier than it says here.' He tapped the stiff, grimy paper of the dodger.

'That's years old — when Brazos first hit the owlhoot trail. Outlaws don't eat all that well or regular, Sheriff. And obviously he must've shaved off beard and moustache.'

Baker scowled now. 'Don't smart-mouth me, Bannon! Says here he had a mess of scars on his chest where some cowman tried to brand him a couple years back for rustling his stock — but your bullets sure made *that* one hard to find.'

Bannon sighed. 'All right. The hell with it. The bounty wasn't the important thing, anyway. I know that man lying there is Birch Brazos. That's good enough for me.'

He turned his bleak gaze onto the two trail men. 'Don't make much difference whether I pick up the bounty or not — because Brazos is gonna stay dead. And if you two want to join him, why, just have at it!'

But as he moved his hand towards his gun, he felt the sheriff's Colt pressing into his back. His own weapon was lifted from his holster.

'No more gunplay in my town, Bannon!' He sniffed and coughed. '*Damn*! I hate the smell of a funeral parlour . . . OK, there's enough doubt here for me to decide this feller likely ain't Birch Brazos. Which means you've gunned down an innocent man, Bannon.'

The bounty hunter said nothing,

27

inwardly cursing himself for getting into this mess. Baker was scrubbing a hand around his jaw while the other two looked on smugly.

'Could throw you in jail, carry out an investigation, charge you with murder, put you on trial — all that stuff. Too much damn hard work. You boys, here, you got a little vested interest in this — how you like to see Bannon outa town for me — 'fact far as the county line?'

Jack Bannon stiffened at the lawman's words and tone. It was plain enough what he was telling these two hard-cases to do — with his blessing.

O'Brien and Burke merely grinned.

'Be our pleasure to give this feller a real send off, Sheriff!' Rusty Burke said happily.

Baker nodded, prodded Bannon towards the door.

'OK. To make it official — Jack Bannon, you get outa my town. *Pronto*! And you boys see him on his way. OK?'

He clipped Bannon across the back of the head and the man stumbled to his knees. O'Brien and Burke grabbed Bannon under the arms and dragged him outside . . .

* * *

He was still groggy when they put him on his horse and led him out of town, folk lining the plaza to watch and murmur, wondering what was going on.

One of the watchers was a young woman with long dark hair falling to her shoulders from beneath a pale-grey bonnet that matched her frock. Her face was in the shadow of the bonnet's peak and she turned slowly to watch Bannon, sagging in the saddle, between the other two riders.

Her hands where they gripped the handle of the shopping basket she held were white-knuckled and she suddenly turned and hurried away.

Bannon came round to almost full

consciousness just after they had cleared town and were well on the way to the line of Santa Fe County.

His head came up with a jerk. There was a swift movement on his left and something hard bored into his side. He swivelled his eyes that way and met the stony gaze of Pete O'Brien.

'No sudden moves, Bannon. We got your guns. Fact, we got *all* the guns. So, you'd be plumb loco to try to make a run for it.'

'I'd be plumb loco *not* to try!' growled Bannon and at the same time rammed his grey gelding into O'Brien's sorrel, smashing backwards with his left hand. It knocked the gun aside and the weapon blasted as O'Brien's fingers involuntarily squeezed the trigger. The bullet burned across the rump of Rusty Burke's dun and the animal whinnied, jerked and spun, slamming into Bannon's horse. The grey whickered and half-reared but was off-balance. It started to go down, righted itself, and Bannon jammed home the spurs. It leapt forward with a protesting snort, drove hard into O'Brien's mount even as he fired again. The lead was wild, but the noise, intermingled with all the other action, set his own horse rearing and side-stepping, stiff-legged.

He had his hands full trying to stay in the saddle and Bannon backhanded Burke as the man finally righted his horse and reached for his gun. The pink-faced man swore, almost fell out of the saddle, but by then Bannon was racing for the line, which he knew was marked by a bullet-pocked wooden sign which meant practically nothing, and the more permanent boundary of a low ridge with a cone-shaped peak rising from the middle — just beyond which lay the valley of the northern Rio Grande.

A six-gun blasted, followed by the whiplash of a rifle and he ducked instinctively, hearing the *blurrrp*! of a close-passing bullet overhead. The next time the rifle cracked, his grey staggered and pulled over violently, head snapping back and catching Bannon in the face. He saw stars and then the world fell out of orbit and sky and sun and brush and reddish earth all whirled around him until suddenly he was brought up against the unbending rigidity of the ground.

By the time the lights behind his eyes stopped swirling and he could breathe reasonably well again, they were on him. O'Brien put a rope on his shoulders and turned his horse, spurring away with a wild yell. Rusty Burke dismounted in time to plant a couple of hefty kicks into Bannon's body as it twisted at the end of the rope.

O'Brien cut loose with a brace of Indian war-whoops, rode in a circle, smashing his mount through brush so that Bannon was dragged over splintered stumps and gum-sticky branches. He rolled and twisted, fighting to get a grip on the iron-bar-taut rope, but he could not hold it with any degree of firmness. His body rolled and bounced and he choked on the dust, his face hammered by a shower of stones kicked up by the horse's heels. He tucked his chin as deeply as possible into his chest and the stones rattled against the brim of his hat, but he could feel it loosening and knew it would be gone in seconds. His mouth was full of mud formed by the dust and grit mixing with his saliva. He tried to spit, gagged at the wrong time and almost choked as it clogged his throat.

He could hear nothing but an endless roaring in his ears, but his body felt every jar and bump and bang. His palms burned away on the rope so his grip loosened. As it did, he had even less control over where his body went and he spun and bounced and twisted painfully until finally he stopped, jammed between a bush with a thick base and a boulder that almost smashed his left hip.

He lay there, semi-conscious, moaning,

coughing, trying not to choke. There was the taste of salty blood in his mouth and then he felt the rope loosening and a boot toe heaved him on to his back. He opened his eyes, but they were too full of grit for him to see properly. Just moving shadows as they worked around him, kicking, hammering . . .

He dropped away into a blackness that totally engulfed him, but just before it did, he thought he heard two fast, cracking sounds.

Like rifle shots.

★ ★ ★

It was no fun coming round. In fact, he tried for what he figured later must have been a day and a half before he reached a level of consciousness that told him he was lying in a bunk in a strange room.

Not that he could see his surroundings properly, but it had to be a strange room because he hadn't slept in any kind of a room for more than six months. He had been living in the wilds, tracking down that son of a bitch Birch Brazos.

The name slipping into his consciousness seemed to clear his head some — and he began to remember.

The long trail had led him to Amarillo where he picked up a hint that Birch Brazos might have joined up with a trail herd under the Jingle-Bob brand, headed for market at Santa Fe; the weary, hungry ride north; the brief chase and saddle fight with a band of Comanche bucks looking for glory and a white-man's scalp; then Santa Fe — and the turn of his luck so that he spotted Brazos bullying his way to the horse trough in the Plaza of the Sun . . .

Which brought him back to those two hardcases working him over at the county line — and with the full knowledge and consent of Sheriff Miles Baker . . .

But what was he doing *here*? And where the hell *was* here, anyway?

He blinked hard to try to clear the grit from his eyes, rubbed gently at the lids, making them water to help flush them. They cleared enough for him to see a coarse blanket strung on a rope across a corner of what looked to be a small log cabin, the mud in the chinks cracked and falling free in places. He felt a hint of breeze against his battered face, even picked up a faint smell of sage. So wherever he was, he had to be outside of a town.

The bunk he lay on was sapling-framed and blankets sewn together under him formed the bed part. He felt straps underneath the blanket so he figured it was a permanent fixture: folk didn't build bunks with rawhide strapping for temporary use. There was a battered chair beside the bed and some clothes piled and folded on it: they looked like his, but had been washed and, he guessed, the rents repaired.

Then he lifted the edge of the sheet that covered him, found he was naked, his lean body scarred and bruised, but there was pale-yellow staining around some of the cuts and bruises and he figured someone had treated them with arnica and iodine.

Jack Bannon cleared his throat and made a harsh gargling sound in the back of his throat which was as close as he could get to a yell.

But it was enough. Soon after, while he was trying to call again, the screening blanket was slid by a slim-fingered hand and a young woman stood there a moment, before coming quickly to his side.

She was dark-haired and wore a grey dress that had seen better days. Her face wasn't beautiful. but it was kind of handsome in a . . . 'worried' way, was the best he could think of to describe it. Blue eyes roved over him without embarrassment as she lifted the sheet and checked his battered body. He felt himself blush, tried to grab the sheet from her.

She smiled and *then* she was beautiful.

But only fleetingly before the smile faded and she was serious again.

'I'm sorry if you are embarrassed, Mr Bannon. Don't be. Once I was a nurse, and I had brothers, How're you feeling?'

She tilted a jug of cool water against his lips as she asked, allowed him a couple of swallows, then straightened, awaiting an answer.

His voice was gravelly, but that water had sure felt great against his throat. 'Like . . . like I been dragged . . . halfway to Hell . . . behind a . . . horse.'

The smile returned briefly. 'It says something for your spirit that you can retain your sense of humour after what happened to you.'

Bannon frowned, remembering. 'Two of 'em. Worked me over — with the sheriff's blessing.'

Her eyebrows arched and he was close enough to see that they had been darkened with some kind of cosmetic pencil . . . actually, they must be naturally golden, he figured, seeing a couple of stray blonde hairs had escaped the sweeps of the dark pencil or brush.

'Oh, I didn't realize Sheriff Baker had sent those men with you to beat you up.'

'Don't like bounty hunters.'

She was completely sober again now. 'I see . . . '

She went silent, looking thoughtful, and was suddenly aware that Bannon was staring hard at her.

'Is something wrong?' she asked tightly.

'I've seen you somewhere before . . . '

'That's not likely, Mr Bannon.' Curt. Edgy.

'You got a name?'

'Of course — but it won't mean anything to you.'

He waited, managing to look expectant despite his blotched, swollen, battered features. She sighed.

'Mary Gordon, if you must know.'

'Well, you're right, it don't mean

anything to me now, but — wait! After I downed Brazos, you were on the boardwalk, in a green and white dress!' He watched her stiffen and he had the impression she was holding her breath, waiting for him to continue. 'But your hair was blonde . . . '

She took a deep breath. 'You have a good eye for detail, Mr Bannon, but then I suppose you had to cultivate that attribute in your profession.'

He smiled ruefully, wincing as a deep cut in his lower lip popped open and began to bleed. She dabbed at it with a piece of clean cotton. 'It is handy. So you don't make a mistake.'

'Like you did with Birch Brazos?'

He shook his head gently and screwed up his eyes as even the small movement made it feel as if his brain was loose in his skull.

'No mistake — that was Brazos, all right. He'd used plenty of fake names in the past. Shaved off his beard and moustache and sideburns, got himself a job with Jingle-Bob McCall in Amarillo as a trail-driver and headed for Santa Fe . . . Those two who claim he was their pard, might just be a couple of hardcases working the cattle trails and took a liking to him. More likely they're old pards of Brazos' and just made things tough for me by claiming it wasn't him I'd killed . . . '

She spoke slowly, nodding. 'I think maybe you're right about that. They were clearly going to kill you out by Peak Ridge when I — '

She broke off and busied herself with iodine, dabbing at the cuts on his face and body.

He reached up and took her slim wrist between his fingers, their gazes meeting. 'Just before I passed out, I thought I heard a couple of rifle shots . . . you?'

She said nothing, pulled her wrist free, poured more iodine on to her rag and continued gently dabbing at his wounds.

He lay back and let her work down his body, frowning slightly, and made

41

himself think about that beating he'd taken at Peak Ridge.

'Why would you take a couple of potshots at O'Brien and Burke?' he asked suddenly. 'Damnit, woman, answer me! There's something mighty queer here . . . '

She pulled the sheet over him, wiped her hands on a damp towel before looking down at him.

'I just did what any good citizen would have done. I saw a man being badly beaten by a couple of hardcases and I intervened.'

'Just happened to be passing?' he asked sceptically.

'Just happened to be taking my afternoon ride out that way. And, yes, anticipating your next question — yes, I always ride with a carbine and a small pistol. There are still wild Indians, even that close to Santa Fe . . . and men like the ones who beat you don't always act like gentlemen when they come across a lone lady rider.'

'Sure not one who looks like you,'

he said quietly and she flushed slightly. 'You took a risk, buying-in that way.'

'Not really. I . . . I'm not much of a shot. I don't like guns, but I managed to put a couple of bullets close enough to spray them with rock dust and — well, I daresay they know there are young Comanche bucks prowling the area. They simply got on their horses and rode off. But the one with the pink face did turn and take a couple of shots at you where you lay on the ground. Luckily for you he missed. And I put a couple more shots over his head . . . '

He drank some more water, not taking his eyes off her. 'Were you a blonde when you fired at them?'

Her blue eyes hardened. 'I had a bet with myself that you'd be one of those foolish men who just has to look a gift-horse in the mouth!'

He laughed briefly, he couldn't help it. 'Don't be so indignant! Lady, I've lived as long as I have by asking questions about things I wanted to know. Where's the sense in *not* asking?

The knowledge has saved my life more than once.'

'Oh? You believe your life is in danger now?'

He shook his head slowly and it still felt like his brain was loose. 'No-ooo. I think you rescued me because you've got a use for me . . . can't be any other reason. We've never met before, and if you keep changing your appearance . . . well, you must be something other than what you appear to be.'

She had gathered her things and leaned back against the log wall. 'And just what do I appear to be?'

'Well, you didn't say if you were 'miss' or 'missus', but I see a faint white mark on your ring finger where you could've had a wedding band at one time. When I first saw you, you had fair hair, pulled up under a funny little hat as I recall, and your clothes were much better quality than the ones you're wearing now. Plus your hair is long and kind of wild and darker, much darker. Like your eyebrows, but you missed colouring a couple of golden hairs. You've no paint on your face like you had when you were a blonde, and no jewellery, where before you wore a kind of choker thing round your neck. A black silk ribbon, I think, and some kind of cameo. In short, Mary Gordon, you've made yourself look mighty different to when I first saw you. And all in a few hours . . . '

'Thirty.'

'What?'

'It's now a day and a half later and we're no longer in Santa Fe. I've had this cabin rented for some time at Glorieta. I brought you here in a buckboard.'

It was too much for him to handle. His head thundered and his vision blurred suddenly. He started to put a hand up to his head, but didn't even remember his fingers touching his face before he passed out again.

★ ★ ★

45

It was dark when he came to, though he could see a little amber light coming around the edge of the blanket strung on its rope. He felt sore as hell, stiffer than before, and he had plenty of tender spots. But somehow he struggled to a sitting position, picked up a glass of water from the bedside chair and drank.

Then he called out.

She pulled the blanket aside almost immediately, obviously surprised to see him half-propped up on the pillows, panting with his efforts. She hurried to arrange the pillows and settle him more comfortably.

'You shouldn't move around like that just yet.'

'Just found that out. Look, Mary Gordon, I'm not in too good a shape right now, but I don't take long to recover. I've had worse beatings than what those two gave me . . . but I want to know what's your interest in this. And what you want of me?'

She was silent, then asked if he was

hungry and he said, 'Yes, but — ', and she went away and he heard dishes and the rattle of cutlery. Beyond the blanket curtain he could see a deal table, some papers and pens and envelopes spread out on it near an oil lamp, log walls with a couple of faded prints tacked to them, a set of old deer antlers on which rested a Winchester saddle carbine, and the end of a frame bunk. He smelled woodsmoke and then frying bacon and he began to salivate when the aroma of coffee reached his swollen nostrils. She brought him a heaped plate of food with a hunk of fresh-baked biscuit on one side, and a large mug of coffee.

He began to eat, intending to ask his question about what she wanted of him after he had finished.

She sat down on the old chair at the bedside, watched in silence for a few minutes then said, 'I want you to take me across some mountains and act as my bodyguard. And I'll tell you now that you'll probably have to kill a few men before I get to where I'm going.' Her voice took on a hard edge as she added, 'But that wouldn't bother a man like you, would it, Jack Bannon? I mean, as long as the money's right? That's what's important to you, isn't it? Blood for hard cash — that's what a man like you would call a fair exchange, I imagine.'

3

Mystery Woman

Dancey was all knotted-up in the belly just walking to the Albuquerque telegraph office.

He had sent a wire to Langford as soon as he had arrived, quitting the train at a run. He now regretted sending off that message — he should have done something positive first, *then* contacted Langford. It wouldn't look good the telegraph coming through and all the news it really contained — despite Dancey's stumbling explanations — was that he had lost the girl.

It was a warm day and his shirt was plastered to him with sweat. Dancey used a neckerchief to mop his face as he stepped into the telegraph office down near the railroad depot.

'Messages for Dancey?' He cursed

inwardly at the gravelly sound of his voice and covered the clearing of his throat by a bout of coughing. 'Damn dust.'

But the operator wasn't interested, had turned to look through the yellow message forms in the pigeon holes behind him. He took one down and handed it across the counter.

'Just came in.'

Dancey took it, nodding jerkily, swallowing as he crossed to the small bench where messages were supposed to be written out on the official forms, and opened the paper. His mouth was dry. Christ! he thought. Here I'm damn near 500 miles away from Langford and he can still put a crimp in my bowels!

He read quickly.

Do the job you're paid for.

It was just signed 'L' and Dancey eased the neckerchief, his throat suddenly feeling constricted. By God, he was a frightening son of a bitch, that Langford.

He screwed up the form, tossed it

at the wastebasket, missed, and started out the door as the telegraph key began tapping out an incoming message. He was almost across the walk when the operator called, 'Hey. 'Nother message comin' through for you, mister.'

Dancey turned and his face was tight, the high cheekbones of his Indian ancestry standing out, the almond eyes slitting some as he clamped his teeth. He waited, took the form, had a little trouble reading the operator's writing.

Just recovered T. Be sure to tell Gail. Repeat, be sure to tell Gail.   L.

Breath hissed through his nostrils. Well, that ought to put Langford in a pretty good mood, anyway.

Now all he had to do was find the woman. And the only place he could start was where he had last seen her. Santa Fe.

★ ★ ★

Mary Gordon was surprised to see Bannon limping out of the front door of the small cabin she had rented just outside of town. He was leaning on a broomstick but had managed to dress himself well enough and he squinted now in the bright sunlight.

It was two days since she had made him the offer of a job. She hurried towards him from the small washing-line she had rigged and on which fluttered some of her clothing.

'Don't over-do it.'

He leaned a shoulder against the door frame. 'I'm more stiff than anything.'

'Have you thought over my offer?'

He stared levelly at her. He had watched her ever since she had made that offer and he had noticed her nervousness which she managed to cover pretty well on most occasions. But now that he was looking for it, he saw it clearly enough: she was jumpy.

'I have to go somewhere. I might as well be paid for it.'

'That's kind of a left-handed way

of accepting.' He shrugged and she said, more quietly, 'You don't seem offended by what I said about your bounty hunting.'

'No.'

'I don't intend to apologize. I only wanted it made very clear just how I feel about such things.'

'Ma'am, I don't really care what you think about me.' She stiffened, mouth tightening. '*I* know what I am and I can live with it. What other folk think doesn't matter a damn to me.'

Her face reddened some. 'You — you're very candid!'

'You mean you aren't?'

A small smile touched her lips, softening them. 'All right. We know where we stand with each other. But if you're doing this just for the money and I'm paying, you'll do what I say.'

'Ma'am, if you hire me as a bodyguard, you'll do what *I* say. Otherwise, you might as well save your money.'

She blinked, stared in a long silence.

'As long as I get to where I want to go safely.'

'And where's that?'

'You don't need to know just yet. When we're ready to go, I'll buy us some mounts and all supplies — including guns for you. I'll tell you along the trail, later, where I want to go.'

He frowned. 'What're you running from?'

'That's more than you need to know, Jack Bannon! Now, you'd best sit down in that chair for a while before you fall down.'

He allowed her to help him to the weathered chair propped against the wall, beads of sweat starting out on his forehead. He sighed as he sat and eased back.

'Guess you don't like towns,' he allowed, gesturing to the open spaces around them and the distant ranges.

She smiled ruefully. 'Actually, I do. It's just that, at the moment, I find it more prudent to stay near the edges.'

'For a fast getaway?' He smiled at the stiff look she threw him. 'And the change of appearance . . . which are you really? Blonde or brunette?'

'If you can't tell this is a wig I'm wearing, then it's a good disguise. Have you come up with a fee yet?'

'Depends how far we're going.'

'I told you — somewhere along the trail I'll tell you.'

'Yeah, if it suits you. OK, we make it this way: two hundred dollars to get you through the ranges safely. If there's any gunplay required — and I live through it — it'll be another two-hundred.'

She watched him in taut silence, then said, 'You're taking advantage of me.'

He shook his head. 'No. I figure whatever your trouble is, you'll pay just about anything to have safe passage over the mountains. My fee covers the full distance, whether it takes us two, three days or a week. The other — well, you said it yourself: I'm a mercenary son of a bitch, I guess.'

She nodded jerkily. 'All right. I deserved that. And I agree to your terms. When do you think . . . ?'

'Day after tomorrow — morning, I'd prefer.'

'Too soon! You won't be in any shape to travel by then.'

'I will. So you can go on into town, arrange to pick up a couple of good mounts and a pack-horse. Make sure the mounts have good strong legs. Speed's not as important as stamina in this. You can pick 'em up tomorrow afternoon.'

'All right. I'm a pretty good judge of horseflesh. And your weapons?'

'Winchester rifle .44/.40 and a Colt Peacemaker in the same calibre. I'll need a holster rig and plenty of ammunition — and a set of small screwdrivers and a file.'

'What on earth for?'

'Factory-tuned guns aren't to my liking. I prefer to make my own settings.'

'You . . . you really know your trade,
I suppose.'

'Had some practice,' he said shortly,
then began to roll a cigarette.

'I'll get dressed and walk into
town . . .'

He didn't look up, didn't say
goodbye when she emerged later in her
drab grey outfit and started towards the
outlying buildings of Glorieta, out of
sight beyond a low ridge of sandstone.

* * *

Dancey uncoiled his long, lean body
from the hard bench in the caboose,
tossed the guard a silver dollar and
stretched before stepping down to the
cinders at the Santa Fe depot.

He paused to look around, bony
hands resting on his twin gun butts,
caught the eye of the ticket seller
and walked across to where the old
man stood in the shade beside the
window. He recognized Dancey and
nodded.

57

'See you remember me. Like another silver dollar?'

'Like five of 'em,' the oldster said, and Dancey's horse face straightened, then he grinned crookedly.

'You greedy old son of a bitch!'

The man rubbed at his elbow joints with swollen, misshapen hands. 'Rheumatics gimme hell all year round, real bad in winter. I have to put somethin' away for the time I need to have off.' He squinted. 'You'd be wantin' to know about Miss Jane Boyd?'

Dancey was sober now. 'Damn right! How'd you know . . . ?'

'Seen her drop off the train on t'other side of the tracks. Then I seen *you* hangin' out a car window this side. Looked to me like she give you the slip for some reason.'

'Keep talkin' . . . you might see that five-dollar piece yet.'

'Could it have a brother?' the ticket man asked tentatively, and Dancey laughed shortly, crowded in close and forced the man against the depot wall.

'It could — and then again, you could be needin' a sawbones long before winter. Don't push your luck, Pop. Tell me all you know about Miss Jane Boyd — and do it fast, do it true . . . Savvy?'

The old man swallowed, feebly pushed at Dancey until the man stepped back. 'She changed her hair an' dress — I might have rheumatics but ain't nothin' wrong with my eyesight. She hired a buckboard an' drove right by the depot here not long after them two hardcases, Burke an' O'Brien, drug that bounty hunter outa town.'

Dancey arched his eyebrows. 'The one downed Birch Brazos?'

'One downed a man he *claimed* was Brazos, but Sheriff din' think so and them two hardcases said he was a pard of theirs, a trail-driver, not Brazos at all.'

Dancey snorted. 'It was Brazos. I seen him a few times an' that was him. Where she headed, the woman?'

The ticket man squinted. 'You don' seem surprised that she put on a dark wig and shabby clothin' . . . '

'Never mind whether I'm surprised or not — where was she headed?'

'Guess you'd have to ask Simmons at the livery. He'd've made some arrangement about pickin' up the buckboard.'

'You mean she never come back here?'

'No. But them two hardcases did, like half the Comanche nation was after 'em. Without the bounty hunter . . . '

'Forget the goddamn bounty hunter. I'm only interested in the woman.'

'Well, like I said, *she* never come back. Nor did the bounty hunter. Dunno if there's any connection but . . . '

'Aaaah!' Dancey grew impatient, pushed the old man roughly and tossed him a silver dollar as he strode away towards the town and the livery.

Simmons was a gossipy man and seemed glad of the excuse to lean on the switch broom he was using to clean out a stall in the back of the livery when Dancey appeared and told him what he wanted.

'Well, sir, I did think I'd seen that woman before, yessir, I was *sure* I had but couldn't quite place her. Now you mention she was really fair-haired and wore better clothes, why, I know just who she be . . .'

'That's one thing you don't know, mister,' interrupted Dancey impatiently. 'And that part ain't any of your concern. All I want to know is where she took that buckboard, and if she had anyone with her.'

Simmons, fat and sweating profusely, blotted his face on his sleeve and shook his head. 'By herself. Had some baggage, coupla cases with leather straps, carpet-bag — oh, yes, and a rifle in a scabbard which she kept on the seat beside her when she drove out.'

Dancey's face tightened. 'Drove out — where?'

'Why, she said she wanted to go to Las Vegas, but I could have someone

61

pick up the buckboard in Glorieta — which suited me fine, because I wasn't about to let no one take one of my buckboards to that hell-raisin' town, Las Vegas. You know, I heard there was a killin' up there that'd chill the blood of an undertaker and you know how they . . . Oh? You're goin'? Well, good luck. Just watch out for them hardcases, though.'

Dancey, halfway to the wide street doors, checked and turned slowly. 'Which hardcases?'

'O'Brien and Burke. Sheriff sent 'em out to send that trigger-happy bounty hunter on his way but they come back with their tails between their legs, tryin' to make folk believe it was Injuns drove 'em off . . . ' He snorted. 'Hell, ain't no hostile Injuns where they was s'posed to be. But it *was* on the Glorieta trail and my bet is that woman put a few shots over their heads . . . '

'Why the hell would she do that?' Dancey was interested despite himself.

'Hell, man! She was right behind

'em . . . and my stablehand, Paddy, who picked up the buckboard in Glorieta, said he seen that bounty hunter, all beat-up to hell, sittin' on the porch of the cabin the woman had hired on the edge of town.'

Dancey's heart was beating a tattoo against his ribs now. 'This Paddy around?'

'Not right now. He's a fairly reliable boy, but a little touched, you know.' He indicated his temple, shook his head. 'Father was a drunk, mother a one-legged whore — you believe that? S'true, and she got more customers than them with two legs. That woman could . . . '

'The hardcases!' cut in Dancey. 'Why've I got to watch out for 'em?'

Simmons had to pause for a minute to bring his mind back. 'Oh, they was in here when Paddy come in with the buckboard. They left for Glorieta right away. Aim to square things with that bounty hunter or finish the job they started on him I guess.' He shook his head. 'Mean as a pair of rattlers with a burr up their asses, them two.'

Dancey swore and hurriedly made arrangements to buy a horse. He cleared town ten minutes later at a gallop, both saddle-bags stuffed with grub. And ammunition for his guns.

★ ★ ★

Bannon watched the dust-cloud coming in from the direction of town and he knew someone was moving fast. It could only be the girl.

He took down the carbine resting on the old deer antlers and checked the magazine, levered a shell into the breech and went to the door. He could see her now, coming around a bend at the edge of sandstone boulders. She was riding one horse, leading two others, both with panniers bouncing. One of them, the buckskin, was an obvious mount, the other the pack-horse, but she had distributed their supplies between them for the ride out from Glorieta.

She was waving frantically as she came thundering up in front of the cabin, hauling rein, the led animals slowing but running past her before they stopped. She flipped their reins loose and, breathless, called, 'Two men are following me! I-I think they're the ones who beat you up!'

He smiled thinly, his eyes going beyond her to the bend by the boulders. 'I hope so.'

By now she had dismounted and was on the stoop beside him, handing him a long parcel. He didn't take it. 'If that's my new rifle and six-gun keep 'em for now. This one feels fine.'

'What am I going to use?'

He glanced at her sharply, then returned his gaze to the bend. 'Nothing. Just get under cover.'

She glanced back towards the low sandstone ridge, saw a little dust lifting above it. 'But . . . '

'I'm the bodyguard, remember?'

'You're not fit for any kind of a fight!'

'Watch,' he said, as the two men came riding in and he recognized Pete O'Brien and Rusty Burke.

The carbine lifted to his shoulder and they saw the movement, wheeled in opposite directions. He took O'Brien first, the shot winging the man in the upper left arm. He swayed in the saddle, snatched at his reins, having to drop the Colt he had drawn, then fell sprawling from the saddle.

Rusty Burke was shooting by then and the girl gasped behind Bannon. He dropped stiffly to one knee, grunting a little, beaded Burke, and his bullet burned across the man's thigh. He yelled and fell sideways, hitting the dust hard, one boot caught in the stirrup. Bannon stood, put three fast shots around the horse's pounding forefeet and the animal shied, broke into a run for the bend, Burke bouncing and banging along behind, frantically trying to lift up and free his boot. Bannon

66

put two more bullets over the racing horse's back as it skidded around the bend, Burke almost obscured now in a cloud of dust.

'Where are you going?' gasped the girl, as Bannon lurched to his feet and stumbled out into the yard.

He didn't answer, limped across to where O'Brien was sitting up, dazed, one side of his face smeared with dust and a little blood. He shook his head, lunged for his six-gun and by then Bannon was up to him, clipped him with the carbine's butt. O'Brien stretched out in the dust. Bannon balanced himself carefully, kicked him solidly in the side, bending the ribs.

O'Brien gagged, face contorting as he rolled away, gripping himself. He got almost to his hands and knees before Bannon hit him again. This time the rifle butt mashed his ear and when he started to get up — reacting with the instinct of the brawler — the bounty hunter clubbed him unconscious.

Panting, leaning on the carbine for

support, Bannon blotted sweat from his battered face and lifted his eyes as the girl came running up, looking horrified.

'My God! You're an efficient savage, aren't you?'

'Just do what has to be done.'

It was only as he limped and stumbled his way back to the cabin that she realized how badly he was still hurting from the injuries the two hardcases had inflicted.

'What're we going to do now?'

'Get out of here.'

She ran after him. 'You can't! You're not fit!'

'Just get the horses ready. I'll set here and watch in case Burke's in any shape to come back.'

She surprised herself when she obeyed without further question.

4

Pursued

She wanted to cross the Sangre de Cristo mountain range. But she didn't tell Bannon that until they were well clear of the cabin and had made their way north through the Glorieta Pass, scene of such bloodshed during the Civil War.

Jack Bannon happened to be watching the backtrail at the time and he looked up slowly, turned to glance up at her. 'I take it you'll be wanting to stay well clear of Santa Fe?'

'Yes.'

She sounded tense and acted it, the way she sat stiffly in the saddle and kept swivelling her head around. She was dressed in buckskin trousers, waistcoat of the same material with some Indian bead-work on it, over a

69

checked shirt. She had removed the black wig, pushed her shorter fair hair up on top of her head and jammed on a battered hat so that at first glance — and even several later ones — she looked like a young man. She had chosen baggy clothes so as to disguise her woman's figure and she wore a Colt .36 in a holster at waist level, in a cross-draw position. She had even pulled on a pair of stained wash-leather work gloves to hide her small hands.

He knew she had been planning this for some time: that kind of outfit wasn't one most people could just pull out of their clothes' closet or carpet-bag.

'What name you using today?'

She glared. 'Don't be smart with me, Jack Bannon! Just remember, I'm the one paying your wages.'

He shrugged. 'You can stop any time — I don't particularly want to go north.'

'Did I say we were going north?'

'We will be if we go over the Cristos.'

'Not necessarily.'

He nodded slowly. 'True — we can swing in other directions. But to cross from this angle, we have to go north.'

'Let's do that then — until we reach the crest. Then I'll decide which way to go.'

He shook his head slowly. 'You're the boss. And quit worrying about the back-trail. I'll cover the tracks so a full-blood Comanche can't find them.'

She was silent for a few yards, then asked, 'How about a half-breed Kiowa?'

He snapped up his head, waiting for explanation.

'There . . . there's a man. His name is Dancey and his father was a Kiowa war chief, but Dancey grew up mostly on a reservation, till he ran off with some wild young bucks and they raided and murdered for years . . . '

'What's a man like that doing trailing you?'

Her eyes snapped at him. 'You don't need to know the whys and wherefores

71

of everything! Just take my word for it — he'll be tracking us. Trying to, at any rate.'

'Well, if he's good, he might find some sign, but I don't think so. I'll take extra precautions.'

'He — If he comes, he'll probably try to kill me.'

'I won't let that happen.'

A faint smile touched her lips. 'You're very confident.'

'It's what you're paying me for.'

'Well, I-I hope you're as good as you think you are.'

He snorted, climbed down stiffly and began covering their tracks, carefully replacing some small rocks the horses had dislodged from their resting places on the climb up the winding trail, filling in the half-moon marks of the horseshoes in soft ground, arranging dead leaves and twigs so that the place looked perfectly natural. The girl watched, growing impatient.

'We won't make much distance if you're going to take so long.'

'Well, depends what you want, doesn't it?'

Her lips compressed. 'You're very sassy! Don't you like taking orders?'

He mounted again, moving the horse beside a low rock and standing on this first before swinging his leg over the saddle. 'More used to giving 'em,' he said enigmatically, and her frown deepened as she walked her horse past him when he gestured for her to take the lead, presumably so he could cover her tracks.

Funny, the way he guided the buckskin with his knees and slight tugs on the reins, he didn't seem to leave many — or any — tracks, she thought. He *does* know what he's about . . .

He was an irritating man, but she was beginning to see she had made a wise move rescuing him from those hardcases . . . instinct had driven her after seeing him in action in Santa Fe. O'Brien had still been unconscious when they had left the cabin and around the bend they had seen Rusty Burke's body. His boot had pulled off and was still jammed in the stirrup, the horse grazing nearby. Burke himself was scraped raw and badly bruised and cut from being dragged. Bannon had examined him only briefly.

'He'll live — which likely means that's one more hazard we'll have to worry about.'

'You think he'll come after us again? With the other one?'

'They followed you to get to me. Yeah, they'll come when they recover.'

'Then perhaps I should have let you kill them after all.' She didn't sound convinced. Just talking, he thought.

He said nothing. Hell, if he'd figured they needed killing he'd have done it. And maybe he'd be sorry he hadn't yet.

They made their way into the foothills of the Sangre de Cristos, Bannon quietly calling directions to the girl out in front.

So far there was no sign of pursuit.

Dancey's horse was near worn out when he rode into Glorieta the sundown of the day Bannon and the girl had left for the mountains.

He asked where he'd find the girl's cabin and was told it was a little way out of town beyond the low ridge — but it would be no use him going out there now.

'Why? It's a half-moon tonight.'

'No one'll be there,' the livery man told him examining the dusty horse. 'Say, you've run this pinto into the ground, feller! Ought to take more care of good hossflesh.'

'Feed and groom him, that's all you need to do,' Dancey snapped. 'Where's the woman gone?'

'Wouldn't know.' The livery man hadn't liked being spoken to in that tone by a half-breed. He began wiping the yellowed, caked foam from the trembling horse, muttering.

Dancey strode out, turned into

the saloon across the street, ordered whiskey and a beer and a steak, then took his drinks to a corner table to wait for the food.

A middle-aged woman brought it to him. The steak was thick with fat and sizzled, smothered in onions, with some boiled potatoes on the side and a sliced tomato.

'Looks good. You happen to know where I can find coupla fellers named O'Brien and Burke, ma'am?'

The woman pushed a strand of her stringy hair back from her eyes, face lined with weariness and hard work. 'Sure, I can tell you — I have to take them their meals.'

She waited and he frowned. 'They're in jail?'

Still she waited and he took out a five-dollar piece, held it up. He snapped it back into the palm of his hand as she reached for it.

'Not in jail — they're in the infirmary. Someone shot them and beat them up, I hear. They sure don't look very spry . . . '

'How'd it happen?' He still held the coin covered in his clenched fist.

'Listen, boy-o, that's all I can tell you. I'll be takin' my money now if you don't mind . . . or, if you do . . . ' She swivelled her eyes towards the barkeep, obviously her husband, who was leaning on the end of the counter, one hand out of sight.

Dancey grunted, flicked her the coin. 'You might tell me how to find the infirmary.'

'Sure and I might.' She tested the coin between her big white teeth, seemed satisfied and said, 'Half a block down, second house along Pickle Street. You'll see the doctor's shingle outside.'

Dancey found it all right, the greasy meal sitting comfortably enough on top of his drinks: it had been better than he was used to, spending so much time on the trail as he did.

The doctor, a tired-looking man of about forty, gestured to the infirmary set up on a wire-screened porch.

'I'll be discharging them tomorrow. Their wounds are only superficial, although Burke's lost a deal of skin.'

They looked at Dancey suspiciously, O'Brien sitting on the edge of Burke's bed, smoking.

'Name's Dancey. Heard you fellers tangled with some bounty hunter just outside of town.'

'What's it got to do with you, 'breed?'

'Dancey,' the half-Kiowa said patiently, mildly. He couldn't be insulted these days: he'd heard just about every form of bad-mouthing over the years and had decided some time ago it wasn't worth expending good energy every time it happened. But he had a long memory. 'Not interested in the bounty hunter, only the girl he was with.'

Burke and O'Brien exchanged a quick glance: maybe there was a chance to make a dollar or two here and they could sure use some money. That son of a bitch of a Santa Fe sheriff had refused to honour the deal he'd made with them because the bounty hunter had got away.

'What's it worth?' O'Brien asked flatly.

'Depends what you can tell me. I want to know what she looked like, what she was wearing, and where she went.'

Burke snorted. His face was mostly covered with bandages and there were also some on his chest and legs. 'Man, we followed her from town after we found out Bannon was seen on her porch — she was wearin' some sorta grey dress, had black hair to her shoulders — '

'But Bannon was waitin' for us,' O'Brien cut in, sounding bitter.

Dancey smiled thinly. 'I can see that.'

'You don't see nothin', 'breed!' O'Brien snapped. 'So, OK, he got the better of us, but when they was leavin', they stopped to check us and I played possum. She was dressed like a . . . well, in man's clothes, kinda.'

'You mean like a young *feller*?'

'What I said. Watched 'em ride out and they headed over the ridge but I reckon they wouldn'ta been comin' back here to Glorieta.'

'No, not likely,' Dancey conceded. 'Best place to head would be for the mountains.'

'The Cristos?' asked Burke. 'Man, that's rugged country.'

'That's why they'd go there.' Dancey stood, took out two double-eagles and held them up — it was Langford's money and he'd told Dancey before he left to spare no expense. 'One each — now. Doc says he's kickin' you out tomorrow. You want to come along, you'll get a double-eagle each sundown . . . and a bonus when we catch up with 'em.'

They watched his face but the meaning was already clear to these two in his words. They'd earn that 'bonus'.

'Better be a pretty big bonus if we gotta do what I think you want us to,'

Pete O'Brien said slowly.

'You up to it?'

O'Brien stood, annoyed that his ability was being questioned by this 'breed. 'You just track 'em down down, we'll do the rest.'

Dancey flicked the coins on to the bed. 'You can have Bannon; I've no interest in him. But I want the girl alive . . . for a time leastways.'

Rusty Burke's eyes suddenly sparked. 'That mean we can have the pickin's . . . later?'

Dancey nodded. 'Why not?'

'Say, feller,' O'Brien said, dropping his insulting tone. 'You got yourself a deal!'

'I'll be back here come sun-up. You be ready to go.'

'We'll be ready.'

* * *

'Damn! That 'breed's good!'

Bannon slid back a little from the top of the boulder where he lay looking down and back up the ravine below. He saw the three riders, the bandaged hardcases holding rifles while they looked around nervously at the surrounding rock walls topped by plenty of brush and trees where a man could hole-up for an ambush. Dancey was down on one knee at the edge of the shallow ford, a dark-skinned hand reaching into the chill mountain stream and pulling up a fist-sized, egg-shaped rock.

Bannon knew it had a small half-moon chip out of one edge, made by the pack-horse. He had tried to hide it by half burying the rock in the gravelly sand under the water, but apparently the Kiowa's sharp eye had noticed that it was a grey stone in amongst brown, water-worn ones and he had picked it out unerringly. He examined it now, held it up briefly towards the hardcases and then gestured upstream and lifted his head towards the rim.

Bannon ducked instinctively, although he knew he was well-enough hidden here. But Dancey had mighty sharp eyesight.

He waited until the three men started their horses walking up the shallow stream and then slid back and down from the rock. The girl was taking jerked venison strips out of some greasy wrapping paper, squatting beside the coffee pot which she had filled at the stream where it tumbled down amongst rocks before spewing over the cliff edge in a lacy waterfall, forming the stream below where their pursuers were.

'Better eat in the saddle and forget brewing coffee,' he told her.

She snapped her head up, then handed him some jerky on which he started to chew. She had lost a little colour. 'They're coming?'

He nodded. 'Already in the ravine . . . must've moved fast.'

'I thought you boasted that a full-blood Comanche couldn't find our tracks the way you hid them!'

'Guess I was wrong. This 'breed — Dancey, is that his name? Yeah, well, Dancey's one of the best trackers I've ever seen. I've covered the tracks of a whole troop in Indian country and got 'em out safely, but this man's exceptional . . . '

He let the word trail off, seeing her looking at him intensely.

'You were a soldier then.'

He hesitated, nodded. 'I thought it was a worth-while profession.'

'But bounty hunting pays better.'

'It does — sometimes. Just as risky though.'

'How long since you left the army?'

'Damn it, lady, you've three killers not a couple of hours' ride from here! Forget the questions and pack up!'

'Why don't we wait for them here?' she asked quietly, and before he could answer went on quickly, 'If they're that close we won't be able to get very far. You won't have time to try to cover our trail.'

'It'll be dark before they get here. We can travel a long way at night.'

'And they'll still come after us. I-I'm

not really one for confrontations, Jack Bannon, but it seems the best way to me.'

Soberly, he asked, 'You know we'll have to fight?'

She nodded, tense now.

'The only way to stop them is to kill them — that 'breed, anyway. Unless you know something I don't and he can be bought off or — '

'You can't buy Dancey off! He's paid too well.'

Bannon's face was hard. 'I wonder just what the hell kind of deal I've gotten myself into here.'

'We've agreed terms. I thought maybe we could just put them afoot. Shoot their horses . . . ' She wouldn't meet his gaze. 'What're you looking at? It seems a good solution to me.'

'It's one. But men like this won't give up just because they get their mounts shot out from under them. It'll sure slow them down, I'll give you that, but that's all. In a few days they'll be back behind us.'

She tilted her chin. 'Well, perhaps then will be the time to talk about . . . killing. If we must.' Her voice shook.

He chewed and swallowed venison, started on his second strip. 'You pack up and take the horses, mine included. I'll stay and handle things.'

She hesitated only briefly. 'All right. I don't really want to be around . . . ' She tilted her jaw at him again. 'After all, it's the kind of thing you're being paid for.'

He nodded. 'That's fine with me.'

She started to pack away the gear, emptying the coffee pot. As she was putting it in the pannier, she turned quickly to him.

'You are only going to shoot the horses?'

'I'm going to stop 'em. *That's* what you're really paying me for.'

She seemed to be breathing faster now. She started towards him, hands clenched down at her side, as if she would say something, her face more earnest than he had seen it so far. But she stopped, ran a tongue over her lips and her shoulders slumped.

'I don't really want any more killing.' She added quickly, 'All right, all right, I know it's really the only way to make sure we're not followed, but — I — well, I've already been responsible for — a man's death. I — '

Her words trailed off.

'That why you're running?' Bannon asked quietly.

She didn't look up, shook her head slightly. 'Not altogether. Never mind that! Just stop them. If you're as good as you claim you'll have me where I want to go before they can organize fresh mounts. Now *that's* what I want. And you just remember, I'm paying, so all you have to do is carry out my wishes.'

'That won't be an end to it. There seems like a lot of hate here.'

She stamped her foot. 'Are you deaf? I just told you what I want done!'

'Relax. If that's the way you want it,

fine. But we're going to have to have this conversation again.'

'Oh, stop wasting time! Please!'

She returned to packing away the gear and Bannon slid his rifle from the saddle scabbard. He had spent two nights working on it by firelight, adjusting tension screws, filing the sear on the trigger, adjusting the foresight and securing the buck-horn rearsight more firmly. It still needed work but it now shot a whole heap better than when the girl had brought it back from Glorieta. The six-gun was tuned to his satisfaction.

He took a carton of cartridges and stood at the base of the boulder as the girl rode out, leading his buckskin and the pack-horse.

Then he covered her tracks lightly — he wanted the visitors to find *some* sign, enough to hold their interest. Then he moved up the slope and found himself a secure place among some rocks surrounded by brush.

He could hear the girl climbing up

through the trees, glimpsed her twice, and then the light became too bad. He listened to the rushing sound of the thin waterfall and when it started to get dark, he heard what he was waiting for. The unmistakable dull, *clunking* sound of a horse kicking a rock under water, belly-deep water, at the crossing just above the falls.

That pinpointed the trio for Bannon and he hitched around, getting the rifle in the direction he wanted, thumbing back the hammer slowly to full cock.

He waited for them to appear, knowing exactly where they would show, and he settled as comfortably as he could, wishing the light was better. Still, those men had all been riding light-coloured horses. He would be able to find his targets all right.

His finger curled on the trigger as the man in the lead appeared. It was Rusty Burke, the white bandages about his gravel-scarred face a pale blur as he forked his grey mount into the area where Bannon and the girl had been planning to make camp.

Then just as the trigger was about to let off, Bannon eased up the pressure.

The next man should have appeared by now, but Burke was leading the second horse by a long rope — and the saddle was empty. As was the one behind . . .

He swore softly. That damn 'breed again! He'd figured out they would likely camp somewhere above the falls for the night and sent Rusty Burke in first — in case there was an ambush. Then, when Bannon fired, he would give his position away and the 'breed and O'Brien would move in or catch him in a crossfire.

He twisted on to his side and moved back swiftly. One hand knocked the cardboard box of bullets off the rock and it clattered, the cartridges pinging as they spilled on to the stones.

A gun blasted to his left and above, much closer than he would have expected: must be the Kiowa, he thought, even as he fired the rifle one-handed in a token return, spilling off the rock and under the brush. The man fired again and the lead showered him with rockdust before whining away into the gathering darkness.

Bannon gathered himself, hoping his muscles wouldn't be too stiff when he started to sprint away.

Then brush crackled to his right and slightly below and a rifle blasted three fast shots, raking his position, forcing him to keep his head down.

'I think I got him!'

O'Brien, yelling excitedly, crashing through the brush as he struggled upslope.

'I musta got the son of a bitch that time . . . '

Bannon fired twice, the rifle whip-lashing among the rocks. O'Brien stopped dead in his tracks, almost somersaulted as he crashed backwards down the slope.

Bannon was moving the moment he pressed the trigger for the second time. And just as well. Dancey, still above him, put a bullet close enough to punch through the brim of his hat. He hurled himself over a bush and landed downslope, slipping and sliding, tumbling over O'Brien's body, sprawling face down into the campsite.

Rusty Burke came charging in, six-gun blasting downwards, trying to run down Bannon with his thundering grey. Bannon rolled, feeling his healing wounds wrench and split open, got the rifle up just as Burke ran his mount almost on top of him. The Winchester blasted and the horse instinctively shied aside, throwing Rusty's aim. The bullet seared his shoulder and he almost fell out of the saddle. Bannon, on his belly now, punched him all the way out with two fast shots.

The man was still falling and the grey was running on when Bannon felt hot iron lash across his left cheek. His head jerked as blood flowed and he saw the 'breed coming down at him, raising his weapon for the killing shot.

Bannon dropped the rifle, rolled,

palmed up his six-gun and thumbed off four swift shots.

Dancey's body slid right down against him, shuddering, wet, gargling sounds coming from his throat.

He moaned as Bannon pushed him off and clambered slowly to his feet. His ears were ringing, but he could hear the girl's horse as she came racing back down the slope to investigate the shooting.

5

'Time To Talk!'

'What have you done!' she said breathlessly, as she reined down her horse and saw the sprawled men.

Bannon was on one knee beside the Kiowa and looked at her over his shoulder.

'This one out-smarted me. Almost nailed me.' He touched the bullet burn on his left cheek. 'By then there was only one thing to do.'

'Kill them!'

'Or let them kill me.'

Her teeth tugged at her lower lip. 'I knew it would have to come to this. It's just that — I haven't led the kind of life that — prepared me for this kind of thing. I've been rather sheltered.'

'You seem pretty tough to me.' Her eyes flashed and he smiled faintly. 'I mean, the way you handle situations. You saved my neck for one thing.'

'Nice of you to finally acknowledge it,' she said snappishly. Then she heaved a heavy sigh. 'They're all dead?'

'The 'breed here's got a spark or two left.'

She pushed him aside swiftly, knelt over the dying Kiowa. 'Why didn't you say! Make yourself useful, and get water and clean rags.'

He didn't move.

She frowned. 'Well, go on.'

'Waste of time, lady. That 'breed's not going to last more than a few minutes . . . ' Her eyes drilled into him and he shook his head slowly, moved away, murmuring to himself.

He returned with some rags and a canteen and she washed the 'breed's dirty face, wiped blood from the body wounds. She grimaced. Bannon was right: the man wouldn't last long. But she needed to talk to him . . .

She flicked water into his face and

he moaned, stirred slightly. She wrung out the soaked rag over his face and his tongue flickered out and licked as the water washed some of the blood off his chin. His dark eyes fluttered open slowly and she leaned forward so he could see her.

'It's me, Dancey.'

He grunted. His lips moved but no sounds came. She leaned closer. 'P-pocket . . . ' He tried to lift a hand towards his shirt pocket but was too weak. She stared down at him.

'Tell me, Dancey — were you supposed to kill me?'

The Kiowa tried to smile, rolled his head to one side, too weak to reverse the motion. 'No . . . No! He — he wants you . . . back.'

Her breath hissed between her teeth and she had lost a lot of colour. She grabbed Dancey by the shoulders.

'What? He — '

'Wants you . . . back.' The man tried to sit up, made a wild effort, his eyes bulging. Then blood ran from his mouth and he slumped, death rattling in his throat. She released him swiftly and stood up, staring down at the dead man. She covered her face with her hands and moved away a few paces.

Bannon watched her, thought he heard a smothered sob, then knelt and felt in the Kiowa's shirt pocket. He pulled out a bloodstained telegraph message.

The stars were bright and the half-moon had just lifted over a spur of the Cristos. He smoothed the paper, turned it this way and that, reading the words through the bloodstains.

When he glanced up, she was staring at him, eyes wet, mouth hanging open a little. He held out the message form towards her.

'Might interest you — Gail.'

She stiffened, stepped back, stared, and then suddenly got control again and snatched the form from him. She couldn't have had time to read it all, he thought later. Just the first sentence.

Breath sighed out of her and suddenly

her legs folded and she fell. Startled, Jack Bannon caught her before she hit the ground, lifted her into his arms and carried her over to a grassy patch. He stretched her out, got a blanket and covered her, rubbing her wrists. She made a small moaning sound and moved her head but didn't come round completely. He pocketed the message and stood up.

When she came out of her faint the three bodies had gone and Bannon was washing down at the stream. He walked back to where she was sitting up groggily, wiping his face with a neckerchief.

'I'll brew some coffee.'

'Thank you,' she whispered, staring blankly into space.

As he got a small fire going and set the coffee pot, he said quietly, 'Reckon it's time we had a talk, Gail . . . or is it Jane? Or Mary? Or Charlotte, or Libby?'

She looked up slowly, frowning. 'How did . . . ?'

'Took the liberty of looking through your valise. Found a heap of letters addressed to all those different names in different towns — but all in the same handwriting: yours. What were you doing? Writing to yourself to help establish an identity?'

She continued to stare and just as he thought she wasn't going to answer, she said, 'How did you know?'

'Not hard to figure out, not when I know you're on the run. From this 'L' that signed the telegraph?'

'Yes,' she answered after a hesitation. ' 'L' for Langford, Evan Langford. He — he's my husband.'

That didn't surprise Bannon — he had already deduced she had been married, taken off her wedding band. 'He the one you tried to kill?'

She was very subdued now and merely nodded. No explanation.

'You're Gail Langford then?'

'That's my real name, yes.' She pushed her hair back and automatically began tying it up on top of her head again so that when she put on her hat she would once more look like a youth.

'And who — or what — is 'T'?' he asked quietly, saw the jerky reaction, the way her mouth pulled down at the corners. Her eyes glistened, and her hands twisted into the grass beside the blanket where she sat.

'You're relentless, aren't you?'

'Like to know what I've got myself into. And I sure don't know right now. You've told me nothing but lies ever since we met.'

'I had to!' She was emphatic, hands twisting together now. 'I knew nothing about you — except you were good with your fists and fast with a gun — and — and cared for nothing but money.'

'You figure that out all by yourself?'

'Damn you Jack Bannon! You're a *bounty hunter*! Every dollar you collect is tainted by someone's blood.'

'Including the ones *you're* going to pay me for killing?'

Her eyes flashed but she was wary now. 'What — what d'you mean?'

'Well, it's clear enough you tried to kill your husband and ran off. Those letters you wrote to yourself under your new names were postmarked all over the place. You've done a deal of travelling. And that takes money. Also, that valise of yours . . .'

'What about my valise?' Her voice was little more than a whisper again.

'The sides are thicker than they should be and it's not as deep inside as it appears from outside — which means you could have something stuffed in the lining and a false bottom. My guess is money. Your husband's money.'

Coffee bubbled and hissed as it spurted brown liquid into the fire. He took it off, got two mugs and poured, giving her time to recover. But he was watching her hand as it fluttered near that cross-draw-rigged Colt .36.

He handed her the coffee and she took it, blowing into it automatically.

101

But her gaze was on him through the aromatic steam.

'I think — I think I'm beginning to wish I hadn't hired you, Jack Bannon.'

'No you aren't. You're *glad* you hired me. If I was just a dumb ranny who went along for the money, *then* you'd be thinking you'd made a mistake.'

'Oh, you have such a high opinion of yourself!'

He grinned. 'Nope. Just stating fact. And you're riled because I found you out, that's all. And I still don't know about this 'T' Langford mentioned in the telegraph. He sure wanted the Kiowa to let you know he'd 'recovered' ' whatever or whoever it is, and the 'breed did that almost while he drew his last breath. I'd say this Langford is a mighty scary son of a bitch.'

She sipped, winced, set the mug down. 'Yes, he is. And I don't mind admitting *I'm* very scared now that I know he's closing in on me.'

'Can we get back to 'T'? *That's*

what's scared you?'

'I think I hate you, but I also think I'm stuck with you. So, I guess now you know some of my secrets you'll raise the price.'

'The money was never important. If it was, I'd have hit you for five hundred bucks just to see you through the mountains . . . and done something more about collecting the bounty on Brazos.'

'Ye-es, I suppose that's true. You're such a strange man, Jack Bannon.'

'Look, either call me Jack or Bannon or even Mr Bannon, if it won't gall you too much, but forget this double-barrelled Jack Bannon all the while.'

She surprised him by smiling, her eyes crinkling at the corners. 'I've managed to irritate you, I see!'

He said nothing, sipped his coffee, scalding his mouth, but stubbornly refused to let it show although skin was burned from the roof.

' 'T' is Terry — my son. He's only five years old. I hid him with friends my husband knew nothing about before I ran off. But it seems he's — tracked him down and — '

She broke off, voice quavering, making an effort to get a hold of herself. Bannon waited, tongue poking at the dangling layer of skin inside his mouth.

'He wants me to go back. This is his way of forcing me to do it, or, at least *not* doing what I threatened.'

'Which is?'

'What did you do with the dead men?'

The sudden irrelevant question threw him for a moment. 'Put them in the rocks and covered them with others . . . now, quit stalling. If you still want me in this, you're going to have to tell me everything.'

She nodded, dabbing at her eyes with a kerchief, blew her nose. 'I think I'm going to have to tell you my story.'

'I ain't going anywhere for a while.'

' 'For a while'. Does that mean you mightn't stay with me?'

'Let you know when you've finished.'

'I-I can offer a little more money . . .' She broke off at his look, then frowned. 'How can you be a bounty hunter and *not* be interested in the offer of more money?'

'I'm not really a bounty hunter.'

'You're certainly known as one!'

'Well, I did track down and capture a few men who were wanted outlaws, but mostly because they could give me a line on Birch Brazos. He was the one I wanted.'

'Because he had the biggest bounty, I suppose!'

'Now you're being childish. No, I collected the bounty on the others because I needed the money to keep on Brazos' trail.'

'Why did you want him so badly?'

'He murdered a friend of mine. Now, leave that and tell me what kind of a mess you've gotten yourself into. Then we'll see what we can do about getting you out of it.'

She looked relieved but covered it

with a sober look, settled herself, managed a sip of her coffee without scalding her mouth, and began to talk . . . Gail Easton had a fine upbringing, although her mother had died giving birth to her.

Her father, Silas Easton, arranged for the best of nurses and governesses and sent her to school in Chicago while he ran his horse ranch in the Laramie Hills of Wyoming.

It was a turbulent time in that wide territory and the army required many horses, so Silas grew rich and thus was able to give Gail the best of everything, But, when she finished her education she surprised him and everyone else by announcing that she wanted to live on the ranch and work there.

It caused conflict, but in the end he gave in, figuring there was time for her to go live in a big city, maybe with her cousins in California, where she might meet a suitable husband.

Then, one hot July day, Silas Easton rode out to check a sighting of a new bunch of mustangs in the wild and rugged Medicine Creek Canyon country — and never returned.

His body, and that of his horse, was found broken almost beyond recognition at the base of a butte known locally as Big Hat.

Gail was naturally devastated, and adding to the stress of grief was the ranch — how was she to run it? She knew nothing about that side of it. Her father had paid her only lip-service, allowed her to go on a few mustang round-ups under careful supervision, and occasionally, he let her ride a half-broken bronco, but that was as far as it went.

She didn't really mind because she loved the open-air life but, at the same time, had spent so much time away from the ranch at schools that she was a little afraid of it: the wild animals, the Indians who still roved the trails, sometimes hostile, the rough men who drifted in and out of the ranch . . .

She had wanted her father to teach

her how to manage the books, hoping eventually to take this weight from his shoulders, but all he wanted for her was a *good* marriage, a secure life, and plenty of grandchildren.

So, when he died, she was really prepared for nothing. Sure, she knew the social graces and how to ride, but he had never allowed her to shoot guns or do anything *practical* around the ranch.

It frightened her when she realized after he was killed that the ranch was now hers — and she would have to rely on other people to help her run it.

Fortunately, Evan Langford, her father's attorney in Cheyenne, came to her rescue, made his accountant available to help straighten out the books and generally looked after everything and smoothed the way for her.

But she still wanted to *know* — to know how to run the ranch, keep the books, hire and fire.

'Not your worry, Gail,' Langford told her. He was a tall, handsome man of about thirty, had seen life as her father would say, and had a charming way with him. 'You have to get used to the idea that you're the boss now, Gail. You want something done, you *tell* someone to do it, or hire it done. There's no need for you to worry your pretty little golden head about such things.' He put an arm about her shoulder, drew her close to him, smiling, showing his white, even teeth. 'I'll take care of the ranch and you.'

She was immensely grateful, but managed to pick up some of the book work and found that she was seeing Langford almost every second day — with queries, seeking explanations.

Privately, she admitted that maybe she was making up these questions just so she *could* see him.

It wasn't long before he was courting her and, sweeping her off her feet with his greater sophistication and experience, they were married six months after Silas Easton's death.

Maybe the old rancher would have

approved, maybe not. He had liked Langford but had figured him for a ladies' man and a bit of a rogue.

It seemed a happy marriage and, busy now with a new husband to take care of, Gail enjoyed life.

The boy was born at the end of the first year of the marriage — Terry — a bright, golden-haired child with a combination of his mother's and father's good looks. Now Gail was really busy, looking after the boy, and she took little interest in the ranch.

It was just before Terry's fourth birthday that she realized she no longer owned the ranch: it was now in her husband's name. He had papers and showed her her own signature where she had transferred the ranch into *his* name only, agreed he should run it his own way and without need for explanation, that she, now a wife and mother, had no further interest in the ranch. She had no recollection of signing it . . .

For the second time in her young life,

she was devastated: she knew she had been cheated and began to recall now Langford's gradual change towards her, his growing coolness and abruptness, his long hours away, sometimes days at a time.

Then the strange, hard-eyed men began appearing.

She knew they were gamblers. Langford set up his 'studio' as he called two rooms of the house that he had comandeered for his private use and they played cards — poker — until all hours. One game went on for two full days and nights and Langford slept for thirty hours afterwards. When he awoke he was in a foul mood and began drinking. When he was in one of his drunken rages, she learned that he had been gambling away all their assets and money. *His* money, he stressed.

Horses she thought were being driven to market, were only being driven to Cheyenne in payment of gambling debts. Ready cash seemed to be dwindling and once — only once — there was a query from the general store about an overdue account. When she approached Langford about it and reproached him for what he was doing, he struck her across the face.

The general-store owner was found in a back street one night, badly beaten and worked over. No culprit was ever brought to justice over the cowardly attack, but after that, the half-breed Kiowa bronc-buster, Dancey, became Langford's constant companion. She heard through gossip that Dancey was Langford's trouble-shooter and bodyguard and that he had crippled one man and gunwhipped two others who had bothered her husband.

Then came the 'big winter game' as she thought of it.

She had retired early while the poker game continued late into the night downstairs in the big ranch house. She was desperately unhappy now and had contacted an old school friend, Prudence Radford, by letter several times. She was afraid for Terry by now: when drunk Langford couldn't be bothered with the boy, shouted at him, smacked his legs, drove him away. Then, when sober and contrite, he smothered the boy in insincere affection. The lad was understandably confused, but Gail was afraid Langford, in one of his black rages, often unaware of what he was doing, might harm the boy. She contacted one of her old governesses who lived in Cheyenne.

Of course, by this time, she was considering leaving Langford herself. But she knew he would not stand for it: he would send Dancey to hunt her down and bring her back. So she began to plan. First consideration had to be Terry. She had to get him away to safety, then try to act as decoy, lead any pursuit away from where Terry was.

Langford knew nothing about Prudence Radford who lived in Winnipeg, Canada. Through their letters — always using 'General Delivery, Laramie', as the pick-up point — Gail had secretly arranged for Terry to stay with Prudence. Gail would try to lead the inevitable pursuit away in the opposite direction — later, when she felt it was safe, coming back to rendezvous in Winnipeg. The pick-up point for Terry would be at Omaha, Nebraska. The old governess, whom Terry sometimes stayed with, had agreed to take the boy there to meet Prudence. But first came that 'big winter game' of poker . . .

She was dozing, almost asleep, when the door of her bedroom crashed back — they had been sleeping in separate rooms for some time. She expected Langford to come reeling in in drunken passion, but instead it was a beefy, cigar-smelling, gimlet-eyed gambler from Cheyenne she knew only as Booker.

'Git your clothes on, girlie,' he ordered in a gravelly voice.

'Wha-what for?' she stammered, still too dazed to think of ordering him out of her room.

'Because you're comin' with me — I

just won you for one week, all to myself.'

She was aghast, sure she must be dreaming. Then he came closer, threw back the bedclothes and literally dragged her out onto the floor.

'Goddamnit, I'm tired! Hurry it up! *Git yourself dressed!* Oh, you needn't bring any extra clothes — you won't be wearin' anythin' once we get to my cabin in the hills . . . '

She screamed and eventually Langford came with two or three other gamblers. They watched her fight Booker and she was horrified more than hurt when Booker slapped her face and Langford did nothing.

'Aw, come on, quit the goddamn drama, Gail!' Langford slurred. 'Booker won you fair-an'-square. It's only for a week, for Chrissakes. I ran outa cash, that's all . . . '

She fainted away then and woke tied up in the back of a wagon on the way to Booker's cabin.

She preferred not to think about

that week of horror and humiliation afterwards and she never spoke another word to her husband. Her chilling gaze made him actually wince a couple of times and he hit her, but all she did was walk into the kitchen and snatch up a carving knife. She turned on him, holding the knife threateningly low and, startled, he backed off hurriedly . . . he never struck her again.

He began the weekly poker games again, but Booker wasn't part of them for some reason.

She got Terry away to Omaha and when she returned to the ranch Langford was in a mighty happy mood: for once he had won, a large pot of several thousand dollars. He didn't even ask where the boy was. Then, when he was asleep, she took the money and her fastest mount and rode off into the darkness. Selling the horse in Greely, Colorado, she took a stage to Denver, then trains that eventually led her to Santa Fe. She found out that Dancey was on her trail but she didn't care:

as long as she could stay one jump ahead and he followed her — away from Terry.

★ ★ ★

That was where she stopped her story, except to add, 'And it was in Santa Fe that I saw your prowess with a gun and decided I could use a man like you for a companion.'

'You left out a thing to two,' Bannon said quietly.

She frowned. 'Oh? What?'

'You didn't tell me how you tried to kill Langford . . . or what you did to Booker.'

'Who said I did anything?' she snapped defensively.

He smiled crookedly. 'I think I'm beginning to figure out just what you would and would not do these days, Gail. Like I said before, you're pretty damn tough and you like to pay your debts. So, what'd you do to those two sonuvers?'

6

Point of No Return

She had thought that Langford was in a drunken stupor when she went into his 'studio' to open the safe. It was double-locked and he always had the twin, brass keys with him.

But she knew where he kept the spare keys and had the door open within minutes of stepping into the room. Shaking, breathing shallowly, Gail knelt and began stuffing the wads of money into her valise, working by the dim light of a small candle set atop the safe itself. She was almost finished, just three more bundles of notes to go, when Langford spoke behind her and almost stopped her heart.

She twisted, fell off-balance, but her shoulder found the open safe door and it kept her from falling all the way. She blinked as he swayed above her.

'Short of pocket-money, dear?'

He had an almost empty whiskey bottle in his left hand and she knew he must have woken up, decided he needed a bigger drink than was left in the bottle beside his bed, and come down here to get it. He tilted the neck to his lips now and drained the bottle.

'You bitch! Think you could steal from me, did you?'

'Why not?' she answered, heart pounding. 'You stole the ranch from me!'

He paused and then smiled, letting it form into a short laugh. 'So I did! Mighty neat, too, huh? Thought you were signing insurance papers on that last herd we sold the army, didn't you? Ah, well, you only have yourself to blame for being so dumb. Now, put back my money and we'll have us a little talk. You've got to learn you can't touch my property without my say-so! Damn it, *put back the money!*'

She winced at his harsh tone and, hand shaking, took the last wad of bills she had dropped into the valise and returned it to the safe. He twisted a hand in her hair, yanking cruelly, bringing a cry of pain to her lips. He shook her, rapped her head against the iron door.

'By *God*, you're going to pay for this! If you think you had a rough time with Booker, you — just — wait!'

On each of the last words, he banged her head against the door again. Her ears were ringing, her eyes felt as if they were rolling around in their sockets. She fumbled out the next wad of money and almost fell. As she did, her shadow moved and she saw the derringer lying on top of one of the ranch books.

She almost laughed. *She* was the one who had made him put that gun in there! She had found Terry playing with it one day — the child had found it in a drawer of Langford's desk. She was angry that the boy might have injured or killed himself and insisted Langford lock the weapon away in the safe.

'All right, all *right*!' he had snapped. 'The kid couldn't hurt himself anyway. It won't fire unless you cock the hammer — like this. He's not strong enough yet.'

'Please! Just lock it away, Evan,' she had insisted and he had done so, shaking his head about the stupidity of women in general.

And he had even *shown* her how to fire the thing! she thought now as she snatched it up and whirled even as he closed in on her, perhaps remembering through his liquor-fogged brain that the gun was in there.

He bared his teeth as he saw the glitter of metal in her hand as she spun and fired in one panicky movement. The ball ripped across his ribs and he twisted away with a grunt of pain, swinging an arm wide. The bottle shattered against the iron safe door and he tried to jab her in the face as she closed her eyes and triggered again.

This time he went down to his knees, eyes showing the whites as the ball drove into his chest. He swayed, dropped the bottle. She was jammed in against the safe now and tried to edge out to one side as he toppled towards her, hands reaching for her throat. She had dropped the small gun, groped wildly for it, thinking to use it as a club. But her hand closed over the neck of the broken bottle and she swept it up, and felt the edges bite into his flesh. He screamed . . .

As his blood spread on the carpet, trembling, hardly knowing what she was doing, she reached into the safe.

★ ★ ★

She was white-faced as she finished telling Bannon the story. 'I-I didn't know if I'd killed him or not — I *thought* I had . . . and ran. Then, Dancey showed up and . . . '

'Langford sounds like a real snake,' Bannon opined.

She watched him roll a cigarette and light up. He flicked his eyes at her. 'What happened to Booker?'

'Who said anything happened to him?'

'You said he didn't appear at the poker games again after you returned from your week with him.'

'He was ill. They took him to Cheyenne and I-I heard they eventually shipped him to Denver. They weren't sure what was wrong with him. Severe abdominal pains, kept him knotted-up in agony, so I believe.'

He blew smoke towards her, but she wasn't looking at him. He almost smiled. 'Booker make you prepare his meals as well as provide comfort for him?'

She snapped her head around. 'Comfort! Well, perhaps he thought of it that way, but there was no comfort in it for me! That man was depraved! He . . . '

'No need for details, Gail,' Bannon broke, in quietly. 'I think I can tell what kind of man Booker was. But what did you do? Put something in his grub?'

She gasped. 'How did you . . . ?'

'Abdominal pains — *severe* abdominal pains. I guessed it wasn't just your cooking. The food you've prepared for us along the trail has been pretty good . . . '

He waited patiently and she fiddled about with nothing in particular before speaking in a low whisper.

'Looking for baking soda in a cupboard, I found a can of arsenic in the back. There was rat dirt everywhere in the cabin and I guessed he'd laid some bait . . . I — '

He held up a hand. 'I'd've done the same in your position.'

Her expression didn't change. 'I-I'd never done anything like that before! I didn't even know how much. I think I erred on the scanty side.' Then she tilted her jaw at him in that characteristic defiant way she had. 'But as far as I know he's still suffering so maybe I chose the right amount after all. Dying quickly is too good for him!'

Then she covered her face with her hands and hurried off into the brush. He sat there smoking and had finished his cigarette before she returned, red-eyed, but more or less composed.

'You've nothing to feel bad about,' he said immediately, but she found something in her bedroll to fuss with so she didn't have to look at him. 'You'd be better off it they were both dead, but you did pretty good. The fact that they're both still living, though, makes it kind of hard for you. It puts you past the point of no return . . .'

She looked at him now. 'You mean I should keep on running?'

'You don't have a choice. Langford don't strike me as the forgiving type: he might want you back like Dancey said, but I wouldn't bet on how long you'll live. Booker's likely no problem: scum

125

like him, even if he recovers, won't do anything direct. Likely hasn't enough brains to figure out what actually happened unless the doctors spell it out for him. Yeah, you'll have to keep running. I hope you had somewhere in mind to go where you'll be safe . . . '

'Of course I didn't! All I wanted to do was stay one jump ahead of them, lead them away from Terry. Now . . . '

She choked a little at mention of the child. Bannon frowned: he could see what was coming.

'Goddamn! You're going back, aren't you!'

'I have too. I can't leave Terry with Evan! My God, I feel like dying every time I think about it!'

He tightened his lips. 'You'd planned eventually to get up to Canada and join him with this friend, I take it?'

'Prudence Radford — yes. I'd hoped to do that after they got tired of chasing me.'

'You really think they would do that?'

'Well, perhaps not, but I-I thought I could eventually shake pursuit and be able to go to Winnipeg.'

'Maybe. But now Langford's got the boy.'

She frowned. 'I can't understand how. Prudence was going to pick him up at Omaha and Miss Birdwood, my old governess, had agreed to take him there for the rendezvous. Then she was going on to Philadelphia to see some nieces and nephews. It's not likely that Evan caught up with her.'

'Could he be bluffing? I mean, he may not have the boy at all. He stressed in that telegraph for Dancey to *tell* you that he had Terry back, but maybe that's only to get you really upset — or maybe just a ploy to get you to go back.'

He saw the hope flash across her face and winced inwardly: he hadn't meant to lift her expectations too high.

Then he saw how her face tightened up and she shook her head sharply.

'It doesn't matter.'

He frowned. 'What doesn't?'

'Whether he has Terry or not. The only way I'm going to find out is to *go* back!'

He saw immediately that she was right.

'Mighty smart, this Langford,' he opined.

'Yes, he is intelligent.' She fixed her gaze on Bannon. 'Will you come with me?'

'To Laramie?'

'Yes.' And when he hesitated, didn't answer right away, she said quickly, 'I'll pay you well — anything you ask. To the limit of what money I have left in my valise, that is . . . less travel expenses.'

He said nothing, then her bosom heaved.

'If . . . if you need more incentive — I, well, we'd be travelling together, mostly away from towns or other people. If you wanted . . . *me*, I . . . '

Jack Bannon stood abruptly. 'You

128

don't have too high an opinion of me, Gail.'

'I'm sorry, but — well, I still see you as a mercenary bounty hunter. If I'm wrong . . . '

'You are. I already told you that.'

'But you didn't explain! A simple denial means nothing . . . '

He squatted again. 'You saw me fight Brazos and then gun him down. I'd trailed him for six months, over a thousand miles because he'd murdered a mighty good friend of mind. Man named Cap Burrows. Fact, he brought me up, found me — washed up on the bank of a flooded river that'd swept away my folks' wagon, drowned them and the rest of the family. Cap raised me for twenty years. I joined the army and I managed to get a good word in on his behalf when he had a heap of cattle to sell . . . got him the contract . . . '

His voice trailed off and he looked a mite dreamy, but then his voice sharpened again.

'I was out with a troop fighting Indians when I got word that Birch Brazos had jumped him along the trail and stolen the money he'd got for the herd. Birch was scum, half-crazy on rotgut booze he drank in the mountains at his outlaw hideout. He shot Cap to pieces and left him to die of his wounds, with a bunch of coyotes howling on the ridge . . . '

She winced and grimaced but didn't interrupt.

'Took me three months to get out of the army, then I went looking for Brazos, eventually caught up with him in Santa Fe. Like I told you before, I did a bit of bounty hunting along the way to finance the hunt, built a bit of a reputation . . . '

Gail Langford was silent for a while and then said, softly. 'I'm sorry. I-I've misjudged you. But, I'd still like you to take me back to Laramie and help me get back my son and — '

'And . . . ?'

Her eyes bored into his. 'And kill

Langford for me whether he has Terry or not! Will you do it, Jack? Please?'

★ ★ ★

The man was deadpan as he rode into the large neglected, ranchyard, worked his weary sorrel over to the corrals and dismounted a mite stiffly.

His head was just above the saddle as he loosened the cinch trap, hard eyes raking the bunkhouse where a couple of rannies watched him curiously while they smoked. Another man was working just inside the barn at some small chore and a fourth man hammered at a horse shoe fresh from the forge. The rider wore twin guns, was almost as wide as he was tall, and walked with the rolling gait of a sailor — which was curious in itself because Lee Sabin had never even seen the sea.

The door of the ranch house opened and a tall, well-built man stood there, his clothes untidy, stubble on his lantern jaw, hair slightly awry. Once he had been handsome, but now the flesh was eroded and sagging and there were dark circles under the eyes.

The jagged, pinkish scar crossing the right cheek from the corner of his mouth to disappear up into the hairline didn't help his looks much, either. Nor did his right ear, which was a mangled mess of scar tissue as if it had been slashed at some time not too long ago.

The brown eyes snapped into focus with an effort and the voice was raspy as he said, 'Come on in, Lee. You made good time.' He rubbed gently at his left side, just above the belt.

Sabin went inside, removed his hat, ran a hand over his sweat-damp, wavy black hair. He turned into the parlour, Evan Langford following more slowly. The rancher moved to the small table next to a cupboard in one corner, sorted through the bottles and poured Sabin a glass of the bourbon that he favoured. Langford tossed down a shot of rye himself, refilled his glass.

'Well? Find out anything? I sort of expected a wire.'

'Saved you money. Figured I had to come back anyway so decided to report in person.'

'Get on with it, man!' Langford was irritable, looked into his glass, hesitated a moment, then tossed it down his throat and poured himself another. Sabin sipped his bourbon, after first studying the colour critically. But he knew Langford kept only the best booze. He hadn't yet deteriorated to the point where he would drink any old rotgut at all.

'Nothing definite, but way it looks, I'd say your man Dancey has gone to the Happy Hunting Ground — and he took a couple of hardcases with him.'

Langford frowned, leaning his hips against the drink cupboard. He recognized his growing alcoholic's need to be within arm's reach of booze at all time, swore silently, deliberately stood and walked across the room to drop into an over-stuffed chair. Asserting himself, proving to himself that he was still in control.

But only just . . .

His hand touched the scarred cheek and ear. 'I sent Dancey down alone.'

'Seems he might've hired a coupla men.'

'Well, that was at his discretion, I guess, but she couldn't kill all three. She couldn't even kill Dancey. He was mighty good . . . '

'Someone did. Look, Mr Langford, I don't have anything definite at all. For one thing, the woman's disappeared. First she was blonde which I gather is normal. Then she was black-haired, a wig or dye I'd guess. Then . . . nothing. She was in Glorieta, then she was gone.'

'Look, I hired you with good money to *find out where she is!*'

Sabin held up a stubby-fingered hand easily, unfazed by the rancher's rising ire.

'Let me finish. Seems she was nursing some feller who'd tangled with a couple of hardcases in Santa Fe. A bounty hunter name of Jack Bannon. He killed Birch Brazos in the Santa Fe plaza . . . '

'I heard about that. But what the hell was she doing with him?'

Sabin shrugged wide shoulders, drank some more bourbon. 'This Bannon quit Glorieta one day. The girl wasn't with him but on the far side of town he was met by a young ranny, mighty slim and shapely, fair-haired near as anyone who saw him could tell. Wasn't much showing under the hat.'

Langford was sitting on the edge of the chair now, hands wrapped tightly around his glass.

'By God it's her! She's pulled another disguise! She was top in her drama class at that ritzy school! Must've been her!'

'I reckon so, too. The hardcases that Dancey hired, by the way, were the same ones who beat up on Bannon. Seems he'd gotten his own back somehow and they were pissed at him, so Dancey apparently took 'em along.'

Langford was sweating now, looking down into his drink, forcing himself to shift his gaze to Sabin.

'And . . . ? What happened to Dancey?'

Sabin shrugged. 'Some bodies were found under some rocks up in the Sangre de Cristos. One was an Injun or a half-breed. Other two were white men — or what was left of 'em was. Wolves or a bear had scattered the rocks and didn't leave much to be identified. But I figured it had to be Dancey.'

Langford swore, downed his drink, started to get up immediately, but, catching Sabin's glance, settled back as if just making himself more comfortable.

'All right — it was Dancey, I reckon. So this Bannon seems to be a tough *hombre* as you Texans would say, huh?'

'He's tough. Him and me — well, we know each other. I did some scouting for the army a while back. Tangled with him once or twice. He was a major, seemed to think I had something to do with running guns and rotgut to the Injuns.'

'Did you?'

Sabin didn't reply, drank slowly, hard gaze raking Langford over the rim of a glass. The rancher heaved up and strode to the cupboard, poured himself a stiff drink, gestured at the bourbon bottle, but Sabin shook his head.

'I'll just get my money and be on my way.'

'In a hurry to go somewheres?'

'Not 'specially. Why?'

'I need to replace Dancey. You've got a good reputation for being fast with a gun — I'll hire you to do a coupla things for me.' Sabin waited for Langford to explain further. 'Go stop this Bannon, but bring the woman back to me. Alive. I don't care if she's banged-up some, but she's got to be alive. Then we'll talk about hiring you permanently as my bodyguard.'

'I don't come cheap.'

'Already found that out,' scowled Langford. 'But that's OK — you deliver and I'll pay whatever you ask.'

Sabin gestured around the untidy room, the varnish peeling off the walls, dust and junk everywhere. 'I don't have a lot of confidence in that, so I'll want a good advance payment before I do anything.'

Langford waved it away. 'OK. Five hundred suit you? Yeah, that opened your eyes, huh? And you never mind how the ranch looks. I've got someone coming to take care of that; you just concentrate on doing the job I want. One: bring her back alive. Two: if she's still travelling with this Bannon, kill him. I wouldn't put it past her to hire the son of a bitch to come kill *me*!'

'OK. We got a deal. Any idea which way they'll come?'

Langford took a long swallow before answering. 'If they crossed the Cristos, I'd say train or stage to Denver, then same to Cheyenne. Likely they'll ride the rest of the way out here.'

Sabin stood, hitched at his gun-belts. 'You telling me all of it?'

The rancher's eyes narrowed. 'All you need to know.'

Sabin nodded gently. 'I don't like surprises that creep up on me and knock me on my ass, Langford. If there's something dangerous you haven't told me about . . .'

'You know all you need to,' Evan Langford snapped. 'Now come into my study and I'll get your five hundred out of the safe.'

When Sabin watched the man kneel before the iron safe in the other room and swing open the door, he was almost tempted to draw his guns, slug the rancher and make a run for it.

The safe held several thick wads of greenbacks. But wherever it had come from, Langford sure wasn't spending it on the ranch.

★ ★ ★

Bannon swore as he leaned back in the shadows and watched the two men deliberately step into the path of Gail Langford.

It was down near the rail depot at Denver and he guessed she had booked a ticket to Cheyenne. Likely these two had been loitering about, seen she had a deal of money in the brocade drawstring handbag she carried and figured to cut themselves a slice of it.

He ought to have ridden out after seeing her here safely once they had come down out of the Cristos. Stupid, but his conscience wouldn't let him. Instead of taking his money and riding off, he had stayed around town, keeping out of sight, watching the girl as she transformed herself from the youth she had looked like when they'd ridden in, into a red-haired mature woman, complete with some padding in the clothes. He still recognized her, but he doubted that anyone else would think she resembled Gail Langford in many ways.

He had been irritated by the way she had labelled him a killer, despite his attempt to explain what had motivated him to hunt down Birch Brazos and then kill him. Seemed she had totally ignored that, stayed with her own first instincts that he was a born killer — and would take a man's life if the money was big enough.

'I'll give you all I have. It amounts to several thousand dollars,' she had said, trying to entice him into agreeing to go with her to kill Langford. 'There may be some more in his safe . . . if his luck's changed at gambling.'

'Stop it!' he snapped. 'Lady, I'm not a cold-blooded killer whatever you think. Sure, I killed a lot of men in the army, Indians and Mexicans mostly, but that was war. I've killed men in civilian life — couple of outlaws, two men who wanted to murder me for my fancy boots which I'd brought back from Mexico at that time, and

Birch Brazos. With the exception of the outlaws, all those were killed in self-defence.'

'But I told you what he did to me! You said he *needed* killing!'

'Yeah, Langford'd be no loss, but I'm not the one to do it. Not cold.'

She was getting desperate, eyes wide, face taut and pale. She moved in and tried to seduce him and while he was no prude, he didn't care for this approach.

So he took his money and she looked up at him soberly, her eyes growing moist. 'What about Terry?' she whispered.

Bannon stuffed his money in his saddle-bags and stood back from his mount. 'Even someone as bad as you make out Langford to be wouldn't be loco enough to murder a five-year-old boy. Good God, every man within five hundred miles would be after his hide.'

'You don't *know* Evan! He's — he's capable of almost anything to get his own way! He's impulsive, a drunk. He acts without thinking. He could harm Terry without even realizing he's doing it!'

She'd been crying by then, shaking with emotion. She got herself under control, swallowed, and added, 'There — he has another man he sometimes calls on to do dirty jobs for him, a very vicious, callous man. Now that Dancey's dead, he might well call upon him. His name is Lee Sabin . . . '

He almost agreed to go with her then. Sabin was a man he knew from long ago. He'd figured someone would have put a bullet in his head long since, but — no. Sabin had been out of his life for years. Something warned him off on this deal. He wasn't sure what but the hunch was strong and he had survived up till now by mostly following his hunches.

'Sorry, Gail . . . '

She refused to say farewell so he simply rode out.

He should have kept right on going

but his conscience had kept him hanging about. He wasn't even sure just what he had in mind by staying, but — if anything *did* happen to the child . . . And with Lee Sabin maybe in the picture. *Damn!* He hurried out on to the railroad depot as the two men accosted Gail Langford.

7

North

He had seen the men around Denver earlier, both tough, trail-hardened *hombres* who would turn a dollar any way they could, honestly or otherwise. Now they were trying their luck with the girl. She was jostled but she pushed back — she didn't lack guts, anyway — but one of them had snagged her handbag and was trying to pull it out of her grip.

Then Bannon came up behind, smashed a clubbing blow down on to the man's reaching arm, numbing it to the shoulder. The man staggered, grunting in surprise, and Gail jumped back, eyes widening when she recognized Bannon. But he wasn't looking at her.

He pivoted on his right foot as the second man moved in. This one was the bigger of the two, as tall as Bannon, slab-bodied, with a mean look that'd make a rattler turn tail. His lips were working as he cursed and a big fist the size of a coffee pot came whistling towards Bannon's jaw.

Bannon blocked it on a forearm, the impact knocking his arm aside, but he still diverted the blow. It tipped his shoulder, turning him slightly so that the right he threw barely scraped the big man's ear. The hardcase spat at him and closed quickly even as the other, still rubbing his numbed arm, moved in and kicked the bounty hunter's legs from under him.

He went down and the tall one stumbled on top of him, taking the opportunity to drop one knee into Bannon's chest. Breath exploded out of his lungs and he saw stars. The one with the numbed arm kicked at his head but the boot took him on the neck instead. It hurt like hell and the bright lights were joined by a new galaxy of whirling planets.

But through the pain and semi-consciousness, he realized he had to get on his feet again or this pair would kick him into little pieces. They closed in, boots slamming against his body, and then there was a thud and the tall one staggered, clapping a hand to his ear. Bannon glimpsed the colours of Gail's handbag as she swung it back and caught the second man in the face. He roared, blood spurting from his nose, and by then Bannon was rolling, grunting involuntarily as he pushed to his feet. The one with the bloody nose shoved Gail roughly aside and the tall one charged back, arms swinging. Bannon met his charge, ducked under the wild fists, hammered a vicious tattoo of blows into the man's mid-section. The hardcase stumbled backwards and Bannon whirled as the other moved in. The bounty hunter took a fist in the mouth and the pain drove him to a blurred series of punches and hooking elbows and lifting knees that put the man down in a moaning, bloody heap. Bannon swayed, breathing hard.

By then the tall one had slammed him in the kidneys and Bannon dropped to one knee. He instinctively rolled and the kick aimed at his spine missed by bare inches. He twisted, caught the boot in mid-air and heaved upwards. The hardcase yelled and crashed on to his back. He was well-versed in rough-and-tumble fighting, rolled to hands and knees and scooped a handful of dust towards Bannon's face. Jack Bannon threw an arm across his eyes, spat some grit, closed quickly.

A knee came up into the stooped hardcase's face and sent him flying backwards, arms flailing. He brought up short against the rear of the depot building and before he could move, Bannon was on him, hammering at his midriff, hooking him in the jaw, driving a forearm across his throat, finally grabbing him by the ears and smashing his head against the logs. The man's eyes rolled up into his head and his knees sagged.

Before he had spread out on his face, Bannon closed on the other man who was still groggy, lower half of his face smeared with his blood. He took one look at the big bounty hunter coming at him and turned, sobbing in a wet breath as he staggered away around the building.

Bannon let him go, stood on trembling legs, tore off his neckerchief and dabbed at his sweat-and-blood-smeared face. The girl was a mite dishevelled, busy adjusting her red wig which had come a little adrift. The tall hardcase was still out to it in the dust.

'I-I thought you'd left town,' Gail said.

'Decided there was no hurry.'

She smiled. 'Of course — I'm glad you were around to protect me.'

'What happened?'

She sobered. 'I think they must have recognized me. They said something about I was worth a lot of money to

149

them.' She gestured to the tall man who was moaning now, trying to sit up. 'He had some kind of paper in his pocket. I didn't see what it was but . . . '

Bannon had the paper in seconds, soggy with the man's sweat. It was a handbill with several crude likenesses of Gail drawn on it with different hairstyles, one blonde, one medium-shade which would be the red hair, one dark.

Langford was offering $1,000 reward for information leading to her where-abouts and subsequent return to him at Laramie. The ink had run, stained his fingers. Printed recently, he figured. 'They must have a pretty good eye to recognize you in that getup,' Bannon opined.

She shrugged. 'I, too, thought it was a very good disguise, but it seems that Evan must have some idea where I am. I-I'm more scared now than I was before, Jack.'

He looked levelly at her and finally

nodded, turned to grab the hardcase as he lurched to his feet. He stuffed the handbill into the man's mouth.

'No money for you, mister. You want to try again, you better have a gun in your hand. Now get!' Bannon spun him, kicked the man in the seat of the pants and sent him stumbling and sprawling. The hardcase hurried away, not looking back. Bannon frowned slightly: he had half expected the man to reach for his gun, or at least curse him, but not to just stagger off.

The girl looked relieved. She placed a hand on Bannon's arm.

'Jack — please. Will you come with me to Laramie now? I-I need you. I don't think I can do it alone . . . '

He felt her trembling through the hand on his arm and before he knew it, he was nodding in agreement.

'Yeah, I'll come with you.'

She smiled brilliantly.

★ ★ ★

Lee Sabin was not in a good mood.

He had lost at keno and also draw poker. Even though he knew this last was a genuine run of bad luck, he had accused the dealer of cheating and forced the man by insults and curses to reach for his derringer.

Sabin had felt a mite better after his twin guns had roared and hammered the unfortunate gambler halfway to the batwings before the man fell in a heap that resembled bloody rags dumped in the drainage pit behind the infirmary. He had reloaded in the fog of powdersmoke in the silent bar, aware of all the wary eyes upon him. When he had turned to the barkeep the man had actually jumped when Sabin addressed him.

'Best bourbon you've got in the house. And *pronto*.'

The man ran a tongue over dry lips. 'We — we don' stock bourbon, mister — just rye.'

Sabin sighed, leaned on the counter and crooked a finger at the barman.

The man hesitated, came forward slowly, swallowing audibly.

'It — it's good rye. Ain't been doctored.'

'Yeah, trouble is I don't like rye.' Sabin's left hand darted out like a striking rattler, snatching the startled man's buttoned collar, smashing him face-first into the bar. The crunch of the breaking nose was loud in the room. The man moaned, sank to his knees out of sight behind the bar. Sabin reached over the counter, twisted fingers in the unkempt hair and slammed his bloody face on to the shelf, upsetting the pan of dirty glass-rinsing water. The barkeep sprawled unconscious in a pool of blood-tinged slops.

Sabin curled a lip, drew his right handgun and shot out the mirror with carefully placed shots: it was clear he had had practice at this kind of thing.

Then, the smoking gun still in his hand, he turned to face the room. Some men were slipping out through the batwings and the side door.

'Next time I come to this dump, this saloon better be stocking bourbon, or it's likely to burn down. You men tell that to the 'keep when he comes to.'

There was a brief jostling at the batwings and a hatless, sweating, red-faced man of middle age pushed in, dragging a long-barrelled Greener shotgun behind. A tarnished brass star dragged at the pocket of his faded shirt. Wary eyes narrowed and the tobacco-stained moustache twitched as he eyed-off Sabin.

'You the one doin' the shootin'?'

'The hell you think?' Sabin demanded, looking down at the smoking pistol in his hand.

The sheriff had seen the dead gambler by now and he swung up the shotgun to grip it in both hands but didn't cock the hammers right away. 'You got some explainin' to do, mister.'

'*Mister!*' bristled Sabin, his simmering temper coming to the boil. '*Mister!*

Don't you know who I am?'

'I know you think you're a curly wolf an' you're gonna cut loose in my town, but that's where you're mistaken, *mister!* This town may be rough, but I run things my way and I don't allow curly wolves to howl in my bailiwick. You savvy that, Texan?'

'Ah! That's a mite better'n *mister* but I'm still kinda pissed you don't recognize me, Sheriff. Here. See if this gives you a clue.' He holstered his right handgun with a swift and deft twirl that placed the weapon expertly in the leather holster. He held his hands shoulder-high and smiled crookedly. 'Now you try and cock that there Greener before I can draw my guns — go!'

The sheriff was taken off-guard, but as the hands blurred down to the pistol butts, he swore and thumbed back the shotgun's hammers.

Nowhere near fast enough.

Two bullets ripped into his body and he was flung halfway through the batwings where he sprawled on the saloon veranda, scattering the onlookers gathered there, blood splashing on to the worn boards. Sabin sighed, shook his head and walked down the tense and silent room still holding his guns. The men in the bar-room scarcely breathed, gave him a wide berth.

Sabin shouldered the flapping batwings and nudged the wounded lawman with a rough boot toe, leaned forward and prodded the man in the middle of his bloody chest. The sheriff was grey-white, stared up with pain-filled eyes.

'You dumb bastard!' Sabin growled. 'I'm *Lee Sabin*! And you didn't even recognize me! You hear what I said? I'm — *Lee* — *Sabin*!'

He spoke with feeling, looked for some recognition in the dying man's eyes, cursed when there was none, stepped over the shuddering body and strode away down Main shaking his head slowly — and still holding his smoking guns.

When he turned into the street that

led to the railroad depot, the ticket clerk hastily closed the window and tried to sneak out the back door of his shack. He stopped running when one of Sabin's bullets sang past his ear.

He was a youngish man, thin and work-worn, hair lank, a little stubble showing here and there where he had shaved with a blunt blade, eyes either side of a hooked nose wide with fear. He thrust his hands into the air.

Sabin leaned a shoulder against the door frame and gestured with his left-hand Colt for the man to approach. When he didn't come fast enough, he shot into the ground a bare inch from his scuffed boot.

'Next one goes right through the middle,' he said, and the man rushed up, stood trembling. 'OK, relax. All I want from you is a little work with the telegraph key. You can operate one, can't you?'

'Yessir!' The man's voice was a bleat and he grabbed at himself involuntarily, badly wanting to empty his bladder.

'We — we have to send messages station-to-station . . .'

'Get inside there.' When they were in the stifling, gloomy shack, Sabin gestured for the man to sit in front of the key. 'You contact your Denver depot; I want to know if a Mrs Gail Langford caught the north-bound train to Cheyenne, whenever it left.'

'Day 'fore yes'ty, afternoon. Ought to be comin' through Fort Collins here sometime this evenin' — '

'Use that key!' Sabin was quietening down some now, for he felt pretty good after giving in to his bad mood. It was a long time since he had allowed himself to cut loose like that and it felt good. He missed the old days when he and the wild bunch would ride into some town and take it over completely for a few days or a week or for as long as they wanted, doing what they liked. Yeah . . . Good times, those.

The nervous operator was clattering away at the key and sat back, smelling strongly of sweat.

'He's acknowledged. Might take a little while to get a reply.'

'Tell him it's urgent.'

The man tensed. 'Judas, I can't do that! He's ten years senior to me.' He swallowed as one gun hammer cocked and, his jaw trembling, he turned to the key, tapped out a ragged message.

Even Sabin could tell by the brief clatter of the reply that the man at the other end was annoyed. 'Tell him there's been a death in the family and she has to be contacted.'

The railroad man did as requested and not long after the reply came through: no Gail Langford on the passenger list.

Sabin swore and the railroad man cringed, whining. 'It — it ain't my fault, mister!'

Sabin stopped pacing, glared, and then caught himself as he started to draw one of his guns again. Hell, what was he doing? Venting his spleen on this poor frightened son of a bitch . . . ?

'Ah, forget it,' he snarled and strode to the door.

The operator couldn't believe his luck. He slumped in the chair and his bladder voided involuntarily. He was swearing and standing, holding his sodden trousers away from his flesh, when suddenly Sabin was standing beside him. He hit the man across the ear, knocking him into the chair.

'You filthy bastard! Listen — you call Denver again. This time ask about a passenger called Jack Bannon. *Do it now*, goddammit! Never mind about the mess — you can sit in that till I'm through.'

The man watched his face when the reply came through: yes, a ticket *had* been issued in the name of J. Bannon for the Denver — Cheyenne train.

Sabin smiled and the railroad man almost fell off his chair in relief. The gunfighter nodded slowly. Yeah — that was using his brain. The girl could be under any name at all and he'd never trace her that way, but if she'd hired Bannon as a bodyguard, then it wasn't likely he would bother changing his name, and if he was travelling on that train, then so was she.

'What time's it due here?'

'Not till seven, eight o'clock tonight. Might be later. But it don't stop here for long. Just picks up any passengers — which there ain't any tonight — and whatever freight we got. And ain't much of that, either.'

Sabin frowned. 'But it will be stopping?'

The clerk swallowed. 'Yeah. There's a little freight, an' — if you want a ticket . . . ?'

Sabin grunted, seemed a mite pre-occupied. 'Where's the undertaker in this dump?'

The railroad man jumped. 'Aw, geez, mister, I got an old sick mother to take care of, honest . . .'

Sabin cuffed him across the side of the head, reached out past the cowering man and ripped out the wiring of the telegraph key, stuffing the instrument inside his jacket.

'Now, let's see if your hearing's improved: *where's the goddamn undertaker?*'

★ ★ ★

The train pulled slowly away from the Fort Collins depot and gathered speed as it rumbled into the night.

In the baggage car it was dark and there were creaks and cracks as the whole kit-and-caboodle swayed and rocked and a few scavenging rats scrabbled around, looking for something to chew on.

But the rats quickly scattered into their hideyholes at a sudden hollow scraping sound: they were always alert to such things. It was part of their built-in survival programme.

The sound came again, louder and longer, followed by a dull clatter and a thump. The rats cringed in their holes, bright-eyes, as the lid of the coffin collected at Fort Collins fell to the floor and a dark shape clambered out stiffly, stretching and brushing fresh wood shavings off his clothes.

He groped his way towards the door, opened it, and started to climb the iron ladder fixed to the side of the rocking car, making for the roof.

8

Killer!

Gail Langford was tired from the long journey and couldn't wait until they reached Cheyenne where she could soak in a hot, sudsy bath.

Bannon, having spent so many years in the army, seemed unworried by travel dirt and apparently was able to doze off if not sleep under almost any conditions. She supposed that was how you were trained in the army when a man simply had to grab what shut-eye he could whenever he was able to relax for even just a few minutes.

But, looking at him now, sitting across from her, facing her, his hat tilted down over his eyes, she wished he was awake and alert.

The closer they drew to Cheyenne the more tense and agitated she became.

After all, Laramie was only a mere forty miles away and Langford had men everywhere who would report to him. She was vastly relieved when no passengers boarded the train at Fort Collins, although she was fairly confident the present disguise was by far the best she had used so far, and that included her stint dressed as a boy or a youth earlier. Thinking along these lines, she instinctively lifted her hand to touch the red wig and make sure it was set firmly and squarely in place.

She smiled slowly, but it was a little tight around the edges. Langford was in for one devil of a shock.

Suddenly, a frown appeared between her eyes and she lifted her head slightly. She thought she heard something on the roof. Her small hands clenched in her lap and she held her breath as she listened intently, flicking her gaze around at the other passengers to see if anyone else had heard anything.

But they were all dozing at this time, except for the old Mexican 'breed, who was smoking a pipe, leaning his head against the window, but his heavy-lidded eyes were partly open. He had crossed himself when they had taken on the coffin back at Fort Collins and seemed uneasy about travelling with a corpse.

She listened hard — nothing.

She kept listening. But there was no repetition of the sound she thought she had heard. Just a light thud — like a footstep? No, she was too jumpy. It could have been anything — even a nightbird landing and hitching a free ride for a few miles. She had seen it happen before.

Slowly she began to relax and, as the minutes dragged by with only the sounds of her sleeping fellow passengers and the rattles and creaks of the train, and there was nothing more from the roof, she slowly closed her eyes and allowed the rocking motion of the car to lull her into a light sleep.

She woke screaming — and with glass showering into her lap.

The noise had awakened the other passengers too, and the dull, wind-whipped sound of a six-gun thudded into the car, drowned by the screams of women and children and the shouts of men demanding to know what in hell had happened.

Then Bannon was hurtling into the aisle and she was dragged unceremoniously out of the seat and thrown to the floor. She cried out as his big body pinned her, shielding her, and his gun blazed, shot out the remains of the window, splintering the frame. The screaming increased and men crouched in the aisles, some with weapons already in their hands.

'What is it?' roared one big miner-type, gripping a sawn-off shotgun. 'Injuns?'

'Dunno,' gasped Bannon, eyes still on the shattered remains of the window. 'Likely is.'

The miner cursed and blasted out two more windows, bringing fresh terror to the huddled people in the car.

As the deafening roar subsided, Bannon strained every sense, heard scraping noises above his head. He rolled off the gasping girl, on to his back in the aisle. He fanned the hammer of the Colt, bullets punching through the varnished veneer and tarpaper of the curved car roof.

He was on his feet in an instant, jumping over prone passengers, thrusting others aside, kicking open the door to the platform. He paused only to reload, dropping a couple of shells, cursing as he shucked fresh ones from his belt loops. The gun fully loaded again, he swung a leg over the rail and grasped the ladder at the side, going up fast, but hunching, pushing back his hat to let it hang and whip in the night wind behind his head. Slowly, he looked up, and ducked as a gun blazed only feet away. Splinters showered him and he changed grip hurriedly, moving towards the front of the car, away from the ladder. He swung free, legs dangling, boots banging against the side of the swaying car.

Sabin, on the roof, his left arm and that side of his face all bloody from splinters hurled into his flesh by Bannon's bullets coming up through the roof, staggered to the end of the car jumped to the next one, a box freight, and sprawled. He rolled, gripping the walk plank with one hand, feeling fresh splinters bite into his fingers. He leaned out and glimpsed Bannon's figure hanging down the side of the passenger car. He fired two shots and Bannon triggered a wild one back but it still made Sabin duck. Then Bannon was heaving up on to the roof of the passenger car, rolling on to the plank walk on his belly, triggering.

Sabin sprawled, grabbed wildly at the walkway edge, missed and slid over. He got a grip on the beading running along the roof's edge and hung one-handed, dropping one of his Colts as his body banged and thumped against the side of the box car. There were cows inside and he yelled as a horn poked through the gap between the planks and snagged his shirt. He wrenched away, lifted his remaining Colt and triggered three fast shots up at the roof in case Bannon was there.

Then a dark shape rose against the stars and he knew the man *was* there was waiting, carefully kneeling and leaning over the edge.

'Should've killed you long ago, Sabin!' Bannon called, words whipped away by the night wind.

'Yeah — you — should — have!' Sabin gritted and triggered again.

But the hammer fell on an empty chamber.

He thought he saw the brief flash of Bannon's teeth. 'Not your lucky night, *amigo*!'

Bannon gripped the roof beading, kicked savagely with his right boot. The heel mashed Sabin's fingers where they gripped the edge and Bannon repeated the blow twice more before

Sabin yelled and fell away into the night.

The train was passing along a ridge and the slopes dropped away from the tracks steeply, dotted with brush and boulders, yards of loose scree in between.

Sabin hit hard, body flailing and sliding as the shale scree slid away beneath him and then he began somersaulting and bouncing away into the darkness . . .

The passengers had crowded back towards the door leading to the platform when Bannon, sweating, smeared with soot from the roof, climbed down.

'The hell was it?' demanded the big miner, still grasping his shotgun.

'Some trigger-happy ranny,' Bannon said, breathing a little hard, looking only briefly at Gail's white face, a small cut on her cheek bleeding a little. 'I got close enough to smell the booze on him, but couldn't wrestle the gun away from him. He fell off.'

He jerked his head over the side

and a couple of women gasped but the miner only grunted.

'Serves the damn fool right. I got nothin' again a man takin' a drink or two to make the time pass, but you can't hold your likker, you deserve all you get.'

He pushed back through the crowd and the passengers, murmuring, went back to their seats. As Bannon drew level with Gail, she touched his hand.

He paused and looked down, whispering one word, 'Sabin. He was trying for me.' He pointed to the small oozing nick in the lobe of his ear that she hadn't noticed until now. She lifted a hand to her mouth.

'He's gone?' she asked huskily, and he nodded again and returned to his seat.

She felt the cool, smoke-laden breeze coming through the broken window and thought how lucky she was. Sabin must have come aboard somehow. *The coffin*! The words came into her head abruptly and she felt a lurch in her belly. Yes, he must have gotten on to the roof, leaned down and looked in each window of the lamp-lit passenger car and recognized Bannon. Or had Sabin's first bullet been meant for her?

No, it wasn't likely that Langford would want her killed now. If he knew about Bannon, more than likely he would tell Sabin to kill the man first.

Luckily the train was swaying more than usual on this part of the run or Jack might've had a bullet through the head.

She shuddered, looked up, caught Bannon looking at her. He was frowning and she forced a smile, lifted a small hand in a gesture to let him know she was coping all right.

But inwardly, she wished the train was going the other way.

It wasn't until they reached Cheyenne that anyone realized the old Mexican hadn't moved for hours.

A close examination showed that the bullet Sabin had fired through the window at Bannon had lodged in the old man's heart, entering from the side.

* * *

The train conductor was angry when he saw the state of the passenger car — none of the shooting or breaking glass had been heard back in his caboose while the train had been travelling. But once it pulled into the depot at Cheyenne it sure was noticed. The conductor ranted and raved and refused to let the passengers off until he had a satisfactory explanation.

Meantime, he had sent a man for the sheriff and when it was discovered that the old Mexican was dead, there was even more furore.

The sheriff was a sour-faced, dyspeptic man named Tatum and he was not happy to have such an investigation thrust at him. But the railroad man was insistent and then Tatum came down hard on everyone who had been in the passenger car, demanding explanations and *written* statements.

'Judas,' breathed Bannon. 'We're gonna be here a couple of days at this rate!'

Gail looked at him sharply, alarmed, face draining a little of colour. 'But that means Evan will have word that we've arrived!'

'You'd best stick to that disguise. Not likely anyone here'll recognize you is it?'

She looked a bit doubtful. 'We-ell, I-I do know Sheriff Tatum. I mean, I know a few people in Cheyenne but I've had dealings with Tatum before.'

Bannon gave her a steady stare. 'That could be interesting.'

'Oh, relax! It was over some horses that were stolen and — well, I stumbled across the rustlers and they chased me and somehow — I-I shot one.' His stare intensified and she added quickly, curtly, 'It was just a lucky shot! I was in a panic and he was out ahead of the others and — '

'Stay with your disguise,' cut in

Bannon as the lawman headed their way. He nodded to Tatum.

'Who're you?' the sheriff demanded.

'Jack Bannon.'

The lawman screwed up his face, looked at some papers the railroad conductor had given him. 'Oh, yeah, the curly wolf who went up on the roof and threw off the other curly wolf who started the shootin'. I'll want to talk to you later. And there'll need to be a written statement. You stand over there. 'Ma'am . . . ?'

He glanced at Gail and Bannon saw her tension and hesitation but the sheriff made no sign that he recognized her. She had used cosmetic paint on her face, the lip-rouge widening and thickening her mouth, eyebrows painted in heavily, and she'd quickly put on a pair of wire-framed spectacles when the lawman approached. Plus there was a dark green veil hanging down from her hat which made it a little more difficult to see her features clearly.

'My name is Carrie Wellings, Sheriff.

I'm a music teacher on my way to an appointment in Omaha. I had the misfortune to be sitting at the window that the . . . the drunken gunman chose to shoot out.'

'How you know he was drunk?'

She indicated Bannon. 'Mr Bannon said so. He struggled with the man trying to subdue him on the roof and smelled the liquor.'

Tatum grunted, staring hard at her now. 'Well, you'll need to make a written statement, too, ma'am.'

'Oh, I'll miss my connection to Omaha if I have to wait around here too long, Sheriff!'

He turned to the conductor. 'Ernie, when's the train leave for Omaha?'

'Day after tomorrow, Sheriff.'

Tatum shrugged at Gail. 'You'll be in time.'

He moved on and Gail, pale, stepped closer to Bannon.

'What're we going to do?'

'Just what the sheriff says, I expect. He doesn't look the type to take kindly

177

to folk disobeying him. Besides, we sneak out, it's gonna look queer and if he has to come after us, we'll be in more trouble.'

Her teeth tugged at her lower lip. 'I'm worried that Evan will get word about us. He must've known we were on the train to have sent Sabin after us.'

'Maybe not. Sabin could've tracked us down somehow but maybe he didn't have time to wire Langford. No, I don't see any other way but to stay put until this Tatum decides he's happy with everyone's story. I heard him telling his deputy to take a couple of men and go back down the line and look for the body of the man I threw off the train.'

She was silent a moment, then sighed. 'Well, we'd better just cross our fingers and hope for the best.'

He nodded. 'At least you haven't been recognized.'

★ ★ ★

Lee Sabin's luck had changed, he reckoned.

It changed in mid-air, while he was falling from the train. For he managed to turn around and drop on to the slope feet-first, facing away from the train.

He hit with a jar that almost put the top of his spine up through his skull, but then he instinctively let his knees bend, taking some of the shock, although it threw him forward. He tucked in his chin, got his head as low as possible and somersaulted on to his shoulders. Then the world went wild, jarring and jerking all over the place as the scree slid out under him and sent him skimming down into the darkness. If it had been solid, stabilized earth on the slope, likely it would have killed him. But the scree sliding away *with* him kept his bones from snapping.

Sure, it tore up his clothes and his flesh and his head banged hard several times. He ploughed face-first through some stunted brush and that didn't do much for his looks. His left arm cannoned off a boulder and there was so much pain he thought he might have snapped the bone. The breath was slammed out of him again and again. He'd no sooner snatch in a lungful of air before his body would smash into some unseen obstacle and it would explode out of him and he would be gasping and gagging until he managed to drag down more air. Then it was repeated — so many times that he wondered if he had somehow found a way into Hell, because it seemed to him that this ravine had no bottom.

But there was a bottom and he was mighty surprised that he was still semi-conscious when he found it. He splashed into shallow water and his face ploughed into wet sand. His body kind of kicked up and over and he flopped on his side, coughing and spitting gravel and water and, by the salty taste, some blood.

But he was alive and through the roaring in his ears, he could hear the distant rumble of the train as it sped on through the night towards Cheyenne.

He sat up groggily, scooped cold water over his face, drank, spat, hawked, and crawled to the bank.

Hell almighty, he was lucky to be alive, all right!

But for a few people still walking around on that train, it was going to be mighty *unlucky*.

★ ★ ★

'What in hell happened to *you*!' demanded Evan Langford calling from the ranch porch as Sabin dismounted stiffly from a shaggy brown gelding and began limping towards the house.

Cowboys working around the yard stopped their chores to stare at the gunfighter.

Sabin heaved himself up the short steps by the rail and flopped into the nearest cane chair. He was sweating, his face blotchy with yellow dabs of iodine, some tape covering a cut above one eye and another on his cheek.

His left hand was covered by a bandage that seemed to disappear up his forearm beneath the sleeve of the shirt that didn't quite fit the barrel body. His Levis were torn and stained and his boots mighty scuffed.

'You son of a bitch!' Langford snarled suddenly, after looking the man over. 'You didn't do the job, did you! You let him get the better of you!'

Sabin lifted his swollen, blackened eyes to the rancher's angry face and Langford backed up a step. 'He won the first round, is how I look at it.'

'Look at it anyway you like, but it means Bannon's still walking around and I guess he's still guarding Gail!'

Sabin nodded wearily. 'I was hangin' upside down from a train roof and it swayed just as I fired at him. Burned his ear, and then I slipped up on the roof and fell off. Lucky to be alive.'

'It don't make me feel good!'

'There was a ranch not far from

the railroad. Feller there used to be in the medical corps during the war. He had some of that heroin they gave the wounded fellers. Since then they've discovered it did more harm than good, but one dose wouldn't hurt he said. He doctored me, gave me a shot of it and, man, I felt like I was flyin' with the birds! For a while — But I rode hell for leather to Cheyenne.'

He squinted up at the rancher. 'Seems my bullet missed Bannon, killed some old Mex. Tatum's runnin' wild with an investigation — be a couple days before he turns everyone loose.'

'Gail's in Cheyenne?' Langford was surprised. 'With this Bannon, I s'pose.'

Sabin nodded wearily. 'I'd sure admire a shot of your bourbon.'

'In a minute. Tell me about Gail and Bannon.'

Sabin sighed. 'Yeah, they're still held up in Cheyenne. Give you a little time to prepare before they come out here . . . ' Sabin squirmed uncomfortably on the chair. 'How about that bourbon now?'

Langford lifted a hand casually — it could have meant anything — while he looked thoughtful. Then he smiled faintly and pushed off the rail where he had been leaning.

'Yeah, OK, Lee. Let's go have a talk about things over a couple glasses of bourbon.'

Sabin struggled up out of the chair, half-hoping Langford would offer him a hand but the rancher merely watched, deadpan.

But he did open the house door and stand to one side, allowing Sabin to limp in ahead of him.

9

The Ranch

Sheriff Tatum was a hard man to please and he was no fool. The way he kept looking at Gail, Bannon was sure the man was suspicious about her true identity.

He made them go over and over their statements, checked out the other passengers, too. But there was nothing he could fault with the information he was given — they all told the same story.

Some drunken cowboy on the roof of the passenger car fired a wild shot through the window, narrowly missing Bannon, the bullet going on to kill the luckless old Mexican.

'Yeah — sounds straightforward,' the lawman admitted, looking at Bannon. 'But thought your name rang a bell somewhere — you're a bounty hunter, ain't you?'

'Not really, Sheriff.'

'Don't lie to me, mister! You passed up this way a few months ago lookin' for Birch Brazos, as I recall. Seems I heard you got him in Santa Fe.'

'That's right.'

'Then maybe that feller on the train was a friend of his, or kin, and he was tryin' to square things with you.'

Bannon sighed, weary of all this. 'Sheriff, I just dunno. I smelled likker on him mighty strong when he grappled with me on the roof. Then he went over the side.'

'And my deputy didn't find any body. Sure, he found marks where someone or somethin' had fallen, but no body.'

Bannon kept his face carefully blank and avoided looking at Gail. But he sensed her tension at this news.

'Then he likely *was* drunk,' Bannon said in a steady voice. 'Drunks hardly ever hurt themselves when they fall.'

Tatum pursed his lips. 'Mmm. Possible. My deputy ain't exactly overloaded with brains. He found some tracks but only followed 'em to a stream. There's ranches out that way. I've sent him back to check, see if any injured man walked into any of 'em.'

Bannon sighed, 'OK. So why're you keeping us here?'

'If the man you threw off the train — '

'I didn't throw him, he fell.'

'Uh-huh. Well, I'd like to check his side of the story.'

Bannon tried to hide his exasperation. Gail wasn't saying anything much and he guessed it was because she didn't want the sheriff's attention on her.

'Look, Sheriff, I have business to attend to. In Laramie. You're costing me money keeping me here.'

'What kinda business?'

Bannon swore under his breath: this happened every time a man told a lie — it escalated each time he tried to reinforce it until it got so complicated it was completely out of control and you didn't know where you were heading.

'I want to look around for some land.'

'Bounty huntin' must pay good.'

'It's not anything that I ever aimed to make a career of — I aim to settle down, that's all.'

'Yeah, well, the land ain't goin' anywhere — nor are you till I say so.' Tatum flicked his gaze to Gail. 'Don't see no reason to hold you any longer, ma'am.'

She stood hesitantly, making sure her veil was hanging in front of her face. 'Thank you, Sheriff,' she said in a small voice. 'I-I hope everything works out all right for you, Mr Bannon.'

He nodded, touching a hand to his hatbrim. She went out and Bannon rolled a cigarette. He lit up and slumped in the uncomfortable chair. It looked like being a long day.

But the deputy returned after sundown, looking weary and scratching at himself as he entered.

'Sher'ff, I found where that feller went to,' he said, stifling a yawn as he dropped into a chair, throwing a casual look in Bannon's direction. 'Staggered into Happy Valley and Sonny Hughes's place. Banged-up some, said he fell off a train goin' to Cheyenne. Sonny sold him a hoss and give him some old clothes, tended to his wounds, some. You recollect Sonny used to be in the medical corps with Reagan's Rangers durin' the — '

'Yeah, yeah, I know all about Sonny an' his bein' a frustrated sawbones. He say if this feller had a name or where he was headed?'

'Man told him he was headin' for Laramie, said his name was Smith.'

Tatum curled a lip. 'Like a dollar for every feller I've throwed in my hoosegow who gave his name as Smith or Johnson.'

Bannon decided it was time to protest. He scraped his chair back loudly, startling both lawmen, stood abruptly.

'Damnit, Sheriff, *now* what're you getting at? So Smith's a common name. So what's wrong with a drifter who says that's *his* name? Judas priest, you've had me here for a whole damn day, fed me lousy coffee and grub, and now that you've confirmed my story, you're still looking for ways to hold me up.'

He leaned forward, glaring coldly at the lawman. 'All right. You either charge me, or I'm walking out of here right now — and if you bring me back, I'll have a lawyer with me. You're outa line, Tatum, and you've just reached the end of it.'

The sheriff remained calm, leaning back in his chair, his hands folded across his belly. He held Bannon's angry gaze. 'Yeah, well, I'd still like to know more, but I guess you're right. There's nothin' I can charge you with. But I can tell you to get outa my town by ten tomorrow mornin'. If you're still here then — '

Bannon held up a hand. 'Save your breath. I'll be gone.'

He spun on his heel and went out into the darkness, hungry, weary and feeling in need of a bath.

In the law office, the deputy stood and stretched, yawning again. 'Me, I'm for supper and early bed.'

'Not yet, Deke. Keep an eye on that Bannon. Tell me if he makes contact with the woman. I smell somethin' here and I still ain't got the right of it.'

'Aw, hell, Sheriff! I'm plumb tuckered!'

Tatum merely looked at the trail-weary man coldly and Deke sighed, reached for his greasy hat and jammed it on his head before lurching out into the night.

★ ★ ★

Bannon met Gail at the Cheyenne Traveller's Rest hotel on Brennan Street, the place they had intended to meet at all along.

'Sabin survived the fall, picked himself up a horse and is headed for Laramie,' Bannon told her. 'Hell,

191

the way that damn sheriff pussy-footed around, Sabin'll be there by now and Langford'll know we're coming.'

Gail tightened her lips, hands twisting. 'I hadn't counted on this. I thought we would arrive and surprise him. I-I don't like him being forewarned.'

'Me neither, but it's done by now, I reckon. You want to give me some money, I'll go get a couple of mounts and some grub and we can move out tonight.'

She thought about it and then nodded. 'Yes, all right. That'll be best. I think the sooner we get there and get Evan out of the way the better. Damn that stupid sheriff and his pig-headedness! Evan could've gotten word I was in town, in which case he'll be ready. I wanted *him* at a disadvantage!'

That probably made sense. But Bannon wondered why she hadn't mentioned the boy — he would have thought that rescuing him was more important than killing Langford.

Then again, to get to the boy, they'd *have* to kill Langford first anyway, he guessed.

But something didn't sit quite right.

★ ★ ★

Deke reluctantly obeyed the sheriff and watched Bannon but he was just too tuckered-out and couldn't stay awake. So he missed Bannon and the girl leaving town — which was just as well because Gail was no longer using any kind of disguise. It seemed unnecessary now that they were this close to moving on Langford — and Sabin.

They quit town in the dark, meeting behind the boarding-house where she had booked a room. She came down wearing jeans and blouse with a calfskin vest over it, and her narrow-brimmed hat. She also wore the Colt .36 in the cross-draw holster and he had purchased a secondhand carbine for her, complete with saddle scabbard.

They left Cheyenne in silence and

took the trail to Laramie. They wouldn't make it by daylight, but they would be far along the way.

They rested in a small draw that Bannon knew, ate a cold breakfast and pushed on before the sun had risen above the Laramie Ranges and spread pink and gold over the mostly flat countryside.

But then it gave way to a series of ridges and hogbacks and the timber thickened, interspersed here and there with huge clumps of boulders, small, narrow passes through the ridges and an occasional creek. They climbed over the ridges at Bannon's suggestion.

'It seems unnecessary,' Gail said, and the tension was there in her voice. She clipped her words and he had come to recognize this as agitation.

'Maybe take more effort, but Langford could've sent a couple of men to watch the trail from Cheyenne.'

She agreed with a jerky movement of her head and he knew she was under a strain now they were getting close.

But he was wrong about Langford sending men to watch the Cheyenne — Laramie trail. The rancher was smarter than that: he put his men amongst the timber and boulder clumps of the ridges, anticipating that Bannon and the girl would ride over rather than use the passes where it was so easy to set up an ambush.

It was on the third ridge. They topped-out, rested the horses a little for it was hot now that the sun was climbing the sky, and then started down, making their own trail. Just before they reached the halfway mark, the two rifles crashed — one in the trees, the other from the clump of boulders.

Gail's horse whinnied and reared as lead kicked dust in front of its forefeet, stones stinging its legs. While she fought for control, both rifles opened up on Bannon and it was clear they were shooting to kill.

He stretched out along the mount, sliding his rifle from the scabbard as he spurred in behind a small cluster of rocks. He quit leather while the horse was still running, lit on a patch of bare ground, breath jarring out of him with a grunt. He wrenched around and rolled into the rocks' protection, lead whining away above his head.

He started to yell for the girl to get under cover, but she hadn't wasted any time, rammed her mount into thick brush in a stand of beech. By the time he had started shooting, her carbine was also cracking but her bullets were ricocheting harmlessly from the rocks where one of the bushwhackers was holed-up.

They ignored her, concentrated their fire on Bannon and he knew Langford's instructions had been to stop him at all costs.

Bannon glimpsed something blue between two sandstone boulders, triggered fast, levered, got off another shot and another, then dropped flat as the man amongst the trees opened up on his cover. There was a yell from the rocks though, and it must have startled the one in the trees, for he stopped shooting and, unthinking, showed his upper body as he yelled, 'Whip? Whip, you OK, pard?'

'No! I'm — hit!' Whip called, the words filled with pain, and before the other man could duck back as he realized he was exposed, Bannon picked him off with a shot that sent him spinning away from the bole of the tree. The man sprawled in the dust, lost his rifle, but struggled to get his six-gun free. Bannon put another bullet into him and crouched, looking towards the boulders. He couldn't see Whip but the man wasn't shooting at him, either.

'Gail, you stay put!' Bannon called. 'Whip might be playing possum.'

'No I ain't! I already done that!'

Bannon felt the short hairs on the back of his neck rise at the words. Then Whip showed himself, or partly — most of him was hidden by the struggling girl. He was a beefy cowpoke in a blue shirt with a blood-flecked rip in one sleeve, no doubt where Bannon's bullet had clipped him without doing much damage.

He was grinning now as he buried his face in Gail's blonde hair — she had lost her hat somehow — one arm about her slim waist, using her as a shield. He held a six-gun in his right hand.

'You'd best show yourself, Bannon!'

Bannon stayed put, said nothing. Whip fired at the rock clump in general, the bullet kicking dust from a lichen-scabbed boulder to Bannon's left.

'I know where you are. I got the gal, you fool! You do what I say or she gets hurt.'

'Langford wouldn't like that,' Bannon called, levering a shell into his smoking rifle.

Whip laughed. 'Bring her in alive, was what the boss said, but he don't mind if she's a mite banged-up. And it'd be a cryin' shame to have to put a bullet through one of them shapely ol' legs, huh?'

He lowered his six-gun, angling it down towards Gail's left thigh. She stopped struggling, her face very white.

'Jack!'

Bannon peered between the rocks, saw how Whip was standing, most of his right side exposed now that he had lowered the Colt towards Gail's leg. He had his thumb on the hammer spur but had not yet cocked the weapon.

Bannon knew if he was going to try anything, it had to be now before that hammer notched back. Once the Colt was cocked, Whip might convulsively squeeze the trigger if he was shot.

Bannon lifted up swiftly, steadied, rifle at his shoulder. The girl screamed and Whip's eyes widened in surprise and his thumb started to notch back the hammer. But Bannon's bullet hit him in the shoulder and smashed his gun arm, throwing him backwards. He dragged the girl with him but she broke away as Whip fell, sobbing in pain.

Bannon was out of the rocks and running forward, rifle covering the writing man on the ground. Gail, pale and shaking, scooped up Whip's fallen Colt and gripped it in both hands, crouching slightly as she cocked it all the way, aiming at him, trying to get a steady bead.

Just as she fired, Bannon reached her and knocked the gun downward with a swing of his rifle barrel. She cried out and gripped her numbed wrist and forearm, turning towards him with blazing eyes.

'Why didn't you let me kill him!'

'You didn't need to,' he told her shortly, shouldering her aside and kneeling beside the grey-faced Whip.

The man stared up at him with naked fear showing through the pain twisting his face. 'Don't kill me!'

'Not yet,' Bannon said casually. 'You'd best see about that arm *pronto* or you'll end up losing it. So answer my questions fast. Where's Langford?'

'Ranch,' Whip gasped, fumbling off his neckerchief and trying to work it over the bleeding wound.

Bannon set down his rifle, took the kerchief from the man and roughly bound it around the shattered shoulder. Whip was almost crying in pain, splintered bone sticking out through the torn flesh.

'Like I said, you'd best not waste time getting to a sawbones. Sabin with Langford?' Whip nodded. 'The kid, too?'

Gail stepped between Bannon and Whip as the wounded man fell back, grimacing, only semiconscious now.

'Come on, we're wasting time! If they're at the ranch and they sent these two to stop us, they won't be expecting us. We should move in quickly.'

Bannon knew she was right, stood slowly, holding the rifle, looking down at Whip where the man lay with hooded eyes and twisted mouth. He spoke to the girl.

'Take a look at the other one.'

She frowned, hesitated, but slid her Colt .36 from the holster and hurried across the slope to the trees. Bannon got Whip's mount out of the rocks and lifted the man into the saddle. The cowboy yelled and thrashed in pain, passed out. Bannon was roping him in the saddle when Gail came hurrying back.

'You killed him,' she said, gesturing back towards the trees. 'What're you going to do with Whip?'

'Set his horse on the trail to Cheyenne and hope it'll walk on into town.'

She nodded. 'It'll find its way, all right. Come on. We have to move!'

They set Whip's horse along the trail to Cheyenne and then rode along the trail to Laramie, figuring that it was safe in this section at least, now that they had taken care of the two men Langford had sent to stop them.

Of course, it didn't mean they were the *only* two he had sent, so they cut back in among the ridges and made their way towards Laramie, skirted the town and, Gail leading now, headed into the wildly beautiful country where the Langford ranch was: timbered ridges, meandering creeks, snow-capped peaks.

There were no more ambushes, but Gail kept to well-screened trails and they came to a bench above the ranch, dismounting and hiding themselves amongst some rocks with brush growing out of them.

Bannon scanned the big sprawling ranch house through his field-glasses, handed them to the girl.

'Someone walking back and forth past the window to the right of the front door,' he said quietly, rifle alongside his prone body. 'Might be Langford. Tall, well-built *hombre*. Couldn't see his face, but the clothes are better than the usual cowpoke's.'

She was adjusting focus, face strained, mouth a tight line as she studied the window. 'It's bad light in that room the way the sun is at the moment . . . Yes! It's Evan!' She paused and he heard her breathing increase a little as she moved the glasses around. 'I recognize those men near the barn, trying to look natural repairing the buckboard. They're just ordinary ranch hands. The one at the end of the bunkhouse, supposedly stitching that cinch strap — well, I think he's a hardcase from town. He certainly wasn't on the ranch payroll when I left.'

'What about Sabin? Or the boy?'

She shook her head. 'They'd keep Terry well hidden. I don't see Sabin anywhere. He might be in the room with Evan, but out of sight.'

'We'd be sitting ducks if we tried to move in across the ranchyard.'

'Yes. But there's timber and bush close to the east end of the house, see? We can work our way around from here and have only a few yards to get to the kitchen door.'

'The cook?'

'A Sioux woman, she's been there for years. I know her well. She won't give us away. And once we're inside . . . '

Her breathing had increased again now and he noticed her hands shook as she gave him back the glasses.

He took one more look, couldn't see anyone with guns, but knew there must be men watching all approaches and that included the east side.

But they had to do something while Langford was thinking the men he had posted along the trail would stop Bannon.

She led the way, keeping to draws and arroyos, bringing them out on a small timbered slope above the east side of the house. They were high enough to look down on the shingled roof. The corrals were at this side, horses milling between the rails. Gail stood watching them as Bannon checked the loads in his rifle and six-gun.

'You'd best check your guns,' he said, and she nodded a little absently. He frowned. 'You all right?'

She didn't answer, kept staring at the corrals. As he stood after ground-hitching his mount, preparing to move down the slope closer to the house, she quickly grabbed his arm.

'Stop! Evan's not there! It's a trap!'

Bannon crouched instantly, whipping his head around towards the girl. She squatted beside him.

'That wasn't Evan at the window! Just someone dressed up in his clothes. Look, he has a favourite horse, an Arab he won in a poker game a year or so ago. He's so damn proud of that beast! Paid it much more attention than he did me. He thinks he's going to make his fortune with it! But — '

'Come on, Gail! Get on with it!'

'Well, it's not in the corrals. No one else is allowed to ride it, or even to groom it. He does *everything* for that horse that needs doing. If it's not there, neither is he!'

Bannon was silent for a time. 'Whip lied, or maybe he didn't. Maybe Langford *was* at the ranch when he left. But if you're right . . . '

'I *am* right, damn you! I know Evan and that blasted horse!'

'All right — where would he go?'

Her face was grim now. 'I believe

he would've taken Terry up to a cabin he has in the hills. He likes to call it his hunting lodge but it's really only a log cabin where he goes in deer season sometimes. It's the only place he *could* go!'

'You know the way, of course.'

She surprised him by smiling crookedly. 'Naturally but there's no way we can approach it without being seen. It's on a rise and commands a wide view of the country on all sides. No one can approach within half a mile without being seen . . . we'd be shot out of the saddle in minutes!'

10

Return

Jack Bannon could see right away that
they weren't going to have any chance
of getting close to the cabin.

It was bigger than the usual cabin,
even if it wasn't big enough to warrant
the term hunting lodge. But it was long
and high-walled and there was a large
enclosed extension built on to the back.
There were a few horses in a corral near
a tool shed, but he didn't see the big
Arab Gail had told him about.

She scoffed when he mentioned it.
'See that lean-to? It's almost more
comfortable than inside the cabin. He
had it specially built for — for the horse!
It's lined and chinked and waterproof.'

Bannon frowned. 'It must be a
damned valuable horse!'

She curled a lip. 'He *claims* it's

worth upwards of fifty thousand dollars — *hundreds* of thousands as a stud stallion.'

Bannon frowned, said slowly, 'Langford's pretty well obsessed with the horse then.'

'That's the exact word! *Obsessed!* To the exclusion of everything — and every*one* — else!'

Her nostrils flared whitely and he watched her mouth tighten as the breath hissed and her eyes narrowed. She didn't care for the horse, a blind man could see that, and he wondered just how much destruction had been brought in their marriage because of the animal.

They were holed-up amongst some trees and the grassy slope leading up to the cabin stretched away before them. Bannon shook his head.

'This open land goes all the way around the knoll where the cabin is. We'd have to be invisible to get up there without having our heads blown-off. No other way that you know?'

She shook her head, face still tight. 'There's no other way. Damnit, I told you, he had it built this way on purpose.'

'Has a lot of enemies, this Langford?'

'Most people hate him. He's underhand, selfish, ruthless once he sets his heart on anything. He simply goes and gets it, does whatever it takes until he has it. Law means nothing to him. He has no compassion.'

'Except for the Arab?'

She snapped her head around and her gaze was cold. 'Are you trying to be funny? Because if you are, I don't find anything humorous in that remark at all. If you'd had to live with — a — rival that's a damn *horse*, how would you feel?'

Holding her angry gaze he nodded slowly. 'Yeah — it would be kind of humiliating.' That bad feeling had intensified . . .

She continued to glare, then said curtly, 'Well? Any ideas?'

He remained silent, looking through

his field-glasses at the cabin. 'No sign of life — wait! Something flashed at the window to the left of the door. There it is again.'

'Looks like a mirror,' Gail said slowly, and then he grabbed her, pulled her back roughly and pressed her to the ground beneath him.

'It's a signal!' he hissed, palming up his six-gun.

She stopped struggling at his words and then heard the scraping sounds off to their right. As Bannon rolled away, the Colt coming around, two men came out of the trees, one with a shotgun.

Bannon shot him first, the man throwing up his arms as two bullets slammed into his body. He staggered backwards, and the shotgun thundered, the charge cutting off young saplings and tearing chunks of bark out of the tree above Bannon and the girl. She gave a startled cry, covered her head with her arms as he rolled up to one knee and fired at the second man who was running, rifle braced into his hip, blasting wildly as he worked lever and trigger. Bannon dropped flat as the bullets flew, bark chips exploding, leaves and twigs ripping up in long lines from the ground. Bannon flopped on to his belly, beaded the man with the blade foresight, led him by a few inches and squeezed off his shot.

The man stopped running as if he had reached the end of a rope tied about his waist. He staggered and the smoking rifle muzzle dug into the soft ground a moment, throwing him around in a slow spiral. His face was contorted with pain as Bannon leapt up, kicked the rifle away and the man fell with a grunt as the support collapsed. He sprawled on the ground, fumbling at his six-gun despite the wound in his side. Bannon stomped on his hand as the gun came free of leather, cocked his pistol and rammed the hot muzzle between the wide eyes.

'Who's in there?' he snapped, and the man stared, unmoving, his eyes very wary and dulled some with pain, but not showing a lot of fear.

'Someone who'll nail your hide — to the — wall,' he gasped.

Bannon smiled thinly. 'Maybe. Some names!'

The man said nothing and Bannon took the gun away, suddenly rammed it between the slightly parted lips, chipping several teeth. He coughed, choked, and gagged, but Bannon kept the muzzle in there until he was still.

'You don't want a cleft palate, you'll answer my question — right now!'

He eased up the pressure as the man nodded carefully. He removed the gun enough for him to talk.

'Langford — Sabin — '

The girl was standing beside them now and she glared down at the wounded man.

'I've never seen this one before!' she cut in. 'He's a hired gun! The whole place seems to be bristling with them. Jack, it doesn't matter who's in there. We're not going to make it to the door!

We might as well go back and think of something else.'

Her words surprised him and the man with the bloody mouth sneered a little. 'There ain't no way you can get closer than this, lady. Langford's had us waitin' in the timber for days, soon after Sabin got back. You show yourself and he'll shoot you both . . . ' He flicked his gaze to Bannon. 'He'll kill you — but not her. He's savin' her for somethin' special.'

Bannon looked quickly at the girl, but her face didn't change and he figured she must have accepted a long time back — when she had first decided to return — that she would be placing herself in a lot of danger. So she had hired him to protect her, had put her faith in his ability to do just that.

Well, they were both still alive, but he hadn't got any closer, really, to getting back her child.

Then suddenly, he swept the gun barrel in a hard, short arc that connected with the wounded man's head and knocked him cold in an instant. The girl jumped.

Her eyes widened and she struggled and cried out as Bannon suddenly grabbed her, yanked the little Colt .36 from her belt and tossed it into the bushes near their tethered horses.

'What're you — ?'

He spun her, one hand twisted up her back between her shoulder blades, as he holstered his gun and picked up his rifle. Then he half-dragged, half-thrust her ahead of him out on to the bare ground between the trees and the cabin. She balked, fear on her pale face now.

'Stop! Have you gone mad!'

'Keep walking!' he snapped, push-dragging her again. Then he lifted his voice. 'Langford! I'm bringing her in! I'm not interested in the whys and wherefores, and I'll shoot anyone else who tries to stop us. All I want is the bounty!'

She stopped dead and he cannoned into her. She tried to turn to get a look at him, but he thrust her hand up and she cried out, half-bending as he shoved roughly.

'Keep going!' he gritted.

'You . . . You — my God, you almost had me fooled! I was halfway to believing you when you told me you weren't really a bounty hunter! Now the money's all that matters after all! You're being a fool! Evan won't pay you anything! Look, you don't understand! *I* had those — '

'You hear me, Langford?' Bannon bellowed, drowning out her words. They were still walking forward, but Bannon was alert, watching for any movement at all from the cabin.

He thought he saw something through one of the windows, back in the shadows of the room beyond, and he tensed, preparing to drop and pull the girl down with him. But there was no reflection of light from gunmetal — just a small movement. Maybe someone with a pair of field-glasses getting a close-up of them as the girl stumbled forward reluctantly, fighting the cruel grip Bannon had on her arm.

They were closer than ten yards to the door when it opened and Sabin stood there, a six-gun in each hand, his bandages showing. He glared bitter hatred at Bannon and Jack tensed, ready to swing the rifle up and trigger one-handed, while he pushed the girl away and down.

But Sabin was shouldered aside and Langford stood there, big and tall, the thin lines of the raw scars standing out pinkly against his tanned skin. He had steely eyes and they rested on Gail who had risen to her toes now, lips forming a compressed rosebud shape as she narrowed her own gaze.

Bannon could almost feel the tangible hate between these two.

Sabin menaced him still, looking impatient, but fighting it, knowing that sooner or later he *would* get to kill Bannon.

'So you're Jack Bannon,' Langford said, shaking his head slowly. 'I'm losing more men since you showed up than I have over the past five years.'

'Then don't send any more.'

Langford arched his eyebrows, laughed suddenly. He glanced at Sabin. 'Sassy son of a bitch, eh?'

'Just tell me when,' Sabin growled, grip tightening on his gun, but Langford flicked a warning finger — not yet.

The rancher was wearing a gun and now dropped a hand to the butt and Bannon tensed. He felt Gail go rigid in his grip as he eased it off a little.

'I've got no argument with you, Langford,' Bannon said. 'Just pay me the reward for bringing her in and I'll be on my way.'

Langford frowned. 'That's twice you've mentioned money. Who told you there was any reward for bringing her back?'

'Your handbills did.'

Langford's face was blank. 'I never put out any handbills.'

Bannon sighed and Gail seemed to be murmuring something quietly, but he fumbled in his shirt pocket and flung the folded handbill he had taken off one of the hardcases who had tried to abduct her at the Denver siding. It landed almost at Langford's feet. Still watching Bannon, he gestured for Sabin to pick it up.

'You pick it up,' Sabin said, gaze unwavering. 'I bend down it'll give this sonuver a chance — and he'll take it! I told you he was mean and quick as a snake.'

Langford grunted, stooped and picked up the handbill, watched closely by everyone as he unfolded it and read quickly. Casually, he turned it so Sabin could see, too.

'Not mine, Bannon. You should read the small type at the bottom. Says 'Printed by Cherry Creek Printery, Denver, Colorado Territory' . . . I ain't been to Denver in three years.'

Bannon was bewildered, then suddenly half-turned the girl towards him, his grip tightening.

'*You* had the handbills printed! What

the hell're you playing at?'

She sighed, spoke to him as if he were a backward child. 'I knew you were still in town: I saw you watching me. I thought I could change your mind and get you to come with me if you thought I was in danger. I paid those hardcases to make a mock attack on me at the siding, gave them the handbills to carry so you'd find one on them.'

He nodded. 'Yeah, I recollect you told me to look in one feller's shirt pocket. Well, I sure fell for it.'

She almost smiled. 'I-I'm glad you did. I don't think I'd be here now if you hadn't come along . . . '

'Oh, sure you would, Gail dear,' Langford said harshly. 'You'd be here, all right. Sabin would've brought you. She played you for a sucker, bounty hunter! There's no money for you at all.'

Bannon said nothing. If Langford couldn't see that he had brought the girl in under his gun as the only possible way of getting close to the cabin without being shot, then the man was dumber than he figured . . . which might be an advantage.

Sabin had worked it out, though, and said so. Langford nodded in reluctant acknowledgement to Bannon who had released the girl now: she was rubbing her shoulder.

'You think fast, Bannon. Maybe you've got a chance of coming out of this alive yet.'

'No!' Sabin snapped. 'You promised me he was mine!'

Langford shrugged, not even looking at the gunman. 'We'll see. She's mighty good at tricking, is our Gail, Bannon. You should've seen what she pulled on me!' He touched his scarred face. 'This was just to ruin my looks. She — '

'You shut up!' the girl snapped. 'I did whatever I had to do to get away from you!' Her hatred seared the air.

Bannon could see this confrontation could easily get out of hand, so he cut in sharply, 'From what I've heard, she had plenty of cause . . . starting with Booker.'

'Booker? Hell, he's not in this!'

'He died?' Bannon asked.

Langford smiled crookedly. 'He did, unless you know some way a man can walk around without his head!'

Bannon stiffened, snapped his gaze towards the girl. She was white, her small hands clenched into fists at her sides.

Langford continued to smile. 'Bet she didn't tell you she set up a shotgun tied to a chair so that when he opened his door — *boom*!'

Bannon frowned. 'Not the way I heard it, but — well, I guess she had cause, after you putting her up as collateral in your poker game.'

'Hell, it was an agreement between gentlemen . . . and *she* wouldn't honour it . . . ' Langford shook his head slowly. 'You got a lot to learn about this woman, Bannon!'

'Jack — he's a master at telling lies and twisting everything around so as to put me in the worst possible light! Don't listen to him!'

'He better if he aims to find out what's really happened up here. You been telling lies, girl. Bannon, she was trying to pull something that would really hit me where I live. After Booker took her, she tried to use him to help her, but he had no interest in it. Hell, I was almost his bread-and-butter, so why would he want to wipe me out? Guess she got scared he might tell me all about it, so . . . ' He shrugged. 'The shotgun.'

'Don't *listen* to him!' Gail stamped her foot, eyes blazing. 'Oh, what's the use! I knew he'd twist things around and make it look bad for me.'

Bannon had had enough of this kind of thing and shot Langford a bleak look. 'Where's the boy?'

Bannon felt the coldness in his belly as he heard Gail suck in her breath and saw the astonished look on Langford's face.

'What boy?'

'Your son — Terry.'

The rancher and Gail were glaring at each other now, only a few feet separating them. She started to speak. Langford suddenly stepped forward and smacked her a stinging blow across the face. She staggered and Bannon's rifle barrel swung in a blur and Langford yelled, lurched sideways, grabbing at his face. Sabin started to lift his guns but Bannon had the rifle hammer cocked and put the weapon on the gunman.

'Go ahead, Lee — and neither of us'll walk away.'

Sabin froze. He wanted so *badly* to kill Bannon, but he knew as soon as he dropped hammer Bannon would fire, too, and, as the man had said, neither would walk away.

Sabin swore softly and lowered the six-guns slightly. Bannon turned the rifle on to Langford who was working a kerchief across his bloody mouth, spitting out a broken tooth. Gail was rubbing at her reddened face, looking murderous.

Langford cut his eyes from her to Jack Bannon. 'I'm tempted to give Sabin the word to finish you, Bannon, but I think I'm going to enjoy giving you the straight of this first. 'Terry' you ask about? Our *son*? That's a laugh! If she'd been able to have kids likely none of this would've happened. She was raped by some friend of her father's, pretty brutally, when she was young. Guess it turned her off men in general. Too bad, because I wanted kids, specially a son . . . '

'You shut up, Evan! You've said enough! You're trying to get his sympathy and turn him against me!'

Gail leapt at Langford, hands clawed, but he caught her wrists easily. He fought her for a moment, then thrust her away, face dark with fury.

'Judas priest! How can you keep up this act! After all this time.' He swung to Bannon. 'Terry's not my son or a child of any kind — Terry is my *horse*, my Arab stallion, the basis of my new stud ranch! She knows this!

That's why she stole the horse. His full name's *Terciado Azucar*. Brown Sugar in Spanish. But I was damned if I was going to have any stud stallion of mine called Brownie — or Sugar — so we settled on Terry.'

'Christ!' Bannon said feelingly, raking his savage gaze over the girl and the rancher. 'This is all about a goddamn *horse*!'

'Hey, not just *any* horse, feller! He's an Arab thoroughbred, and he'll sire the most beautiful horses you'll ever see. Man, he'll be worth hundreds of thousands to me!'

'You're dreaming!' Bannon said. 'You think anyone out here would pay that kind of money for a horse? All they want is something that'll outrun a band of renegade Indians, cut cattle out of the herd and swim a river in flood. They want *working* mounts, not fancy, blood-line stock.'

Langford sneered. 'Typical short-sightedness! Like every damn rancher in the territory! You think I don't know

226

how to spread my wings? *I* know plenty of rich folk in Boston and Washington and Philadelphia who have stables of fine horses. All I have to do is prove that Terry's a top stud and they'll be shipping their dams out here by the trainload! Terry's only the start. I'm already accumulating money to bring in other studs just like him. It'll take a few years, sure, but I've got the time . . . ' He tilted his jaw, half-smiling. 'I'm likely the first visionary you've ever met, Bannon.'

The girl was silent, angrily silent, stewing as her fury boiled within her. Even Sabin looked a little awe-struck by the revelation about Terry. *Hell's teeth*! A damn *horse* could spark hatred like this?

Bannon addressed Gail bitterly. 'It was the one thing he wanted most so you stole it. I see why you've lied to me all down the line now. I must've been plumb *loco* to fall for it!'

'I *had* to, Jack!' she told him earnestly. 'I wanted you to help me,

227

especially after I'd seen you take care of Birch Brazos.' Her face and voice were pleading now. 'I *needed* a man like you, Jack! D'you think you'd've even given me a hearing if you'd known it was about a damned horse? I *had* to make up a believable story to get you interested. I was certain the money angle would clinch it, but you — you weren't just a cold-blooded bounty hunter as I first thought. Then I thought if I said I had a *child*.'

His look made her stop. His face was rock hard, his manner unbending. 'I've killed men to protect you, Gail. Maybe they needed killing, maybe the world's a better place without them, but you lied to me . . . and I fell for it and killed those men because you had me believing a young boy's life was at stake. That *that* was why you wanted to come back!'

'Well, it worked, didn't it?' she said suddenly. 'You came. You protected me and here we are.'

'Now what?' Bannon snapped. 'I'm

all I through being used, Gail.'

'Now, she's gonna pay for all the trouble she's caused me!' Langford said. 'I still dunno how she managed to get Terry away but she did and it was only by pure luck I got on his trail: a dealer I know spotted him planted amongst a bunch of half-broke mustangs on Booker's old spread back in the hills. She talked the foreman into taking Terry in — or got into bed with him or something.'

Gail met his hostile look but said nothing.

'And what've you got planned for me?' Bannon asked.

Langford spread his arms, confident. 'You're Sabin's, bounty hunter. He can do what he likes with you. I got no use for you. You've been a pain in my butt ever since you hired-out to Gail, but you mean nothing to me. She's the one tried to ruin me. Aimed to make me pay for all the troubles we've had over the years. Her idea of stealing the horse was to make me buy him back at a price that'd ruin me.'

Bannon shook his head disbelievingly. 'I hope God threw away the moulds when he made you two!' He was playing for time now, aware that Sabin was just as likely to shoot him down without giving him a chance as not. 'You're no more than a parasite, Langford.'

The rancher flushed. 'A *smart* one, though! Being her father's attorney, I saw a chance to get my hands on the ranch, is all. So I married Gail, and the law says what belongs to the wife becomes the husband's upon marriage . . . that is the law, Bannon.'

'Yeah, I've heard about it. Never figured it was fair though. So what it comes down to, you stole her share of the ranch by marrying her.'

'Not *stole*, you damn fool! It's the *law*! It became mine as soon as she said 'I do', but she didn't like it at all!'

'And you gambled the money away! Almost ruined all that my father had built up before you came along, and somehow talked him into hiring you as his attorney!' She could hardly speak for emotion. 'You wouldn't give me any money. You kept me poor and confined because of it! You stole my inheritance, damn you!'

'And *you* stole my winnings from me! Then tried to get the ranch back by stealing my Ay-rab!'

'So that was to be the price for returning the horse,' Bannon said. 'The ranch — and me along as bodyguard.'

'It's rightfully mine! I don't give a damn for that iniquitous law! There're moves afoot to have it changed, but I saw a way to get my ranch back and I took it!' She softened her face as she spoke to Bannon. 'Surely you can't blame me for that, Jack!'

He shook his head. 'Don't blame you for trying, Gail, but I blame you for getting a lot of men killed. And for shooting Booker so cold-bloodedly.'

'I didn't mean to *kill* him, just to frighten him into helping me. I thought I had the gun aimed above his head but — well, I didn't allow for the weight of the buckshot and its spread . . . '

'Too late for Booker — and it's too late for anything else but to finish this!' snapped Langford, suddenly angry. 'Sabin, kill this son of a bitch while I settle some things with Gail . . . '

Sabin grinned — and holstered his guns, hands still on the butts.

'Don't look so surprised, Bannon. Killin' you is OK, but I'd rather know I beat you to the draw *then* did it!'

Sabin started his draw as soon as he finished speaking and Bannon hurled himself sideways, shooting the rifle one-handed in mid-air. The shot missed, but it threw Sabin's aim and his twin bullets whipped above Bannon's head. He lit on his shoulders, rolled, brought the rifle across his body as Sabin's guns roared again and lead kicked gravel into his face.

His second bullet was wild but then he had stopped rolling, came up to one knee, levering as he lifted the rifle a shade, firing a split second before Sabin.

The gunfighter grunted as lead took him in the chest, driving him backwards, and Bannon put two more shots into him as he spun and collapsed untidily.

Then a bullet smashed into his shoulder and spun Bannon on to his back. He saw Langford drawing another bead on him as the girl flung a handful of gravel into her husband's face. The bullet missed Bannon as he lunged forward and Langford tripped over Sabin's body, fell sprawling.

Bannon's left arm was dangling, blood dribbling from his numbed fingertips, but he kicked the gun out of the rancher's hand. Gail instantly caught it in mid-air, holding it firmly in both hands as she cocked the hammer, aiming at her husband who was blinking to clear his vision. He froze when he saw her cold face above the menacing pistol.

'Gail! Don't!' yelled Bannon, swaying slightly.

She glanced at him wildly, hesitated

and then smiled crookedly. She lowered the hammer. 'No — no. I don't want him to die just yet!'

Bannon watched, puzzled, as she turned and ran down the side of the cabin and disappeared around the rear corner.

'Christ! Stop her!' the rancher yelled.

Langford lunged for Bannon's rifle and Bannon stepped back nimbly enough and brought up the butt, catching the rancher under the jaw. Langford fell to hands and knees, head hanging, blood dripping from his mouth.

Then Bannon heard the dull shot from the rear of the cabin.

Frowning, he ran staggeringly down the side, using the logs occasionally to steady himself. He rounded the corner, light-headed now, and stopped dead in his tracks.

A big, brown, velvety-looking Arab horse lay kicking its last on the ground beside the lean-to, a fresh, raw bullet wound in its head. A white-faced

Gail held Langford's smoking six-gun, looked wild-eyed at Bannon.

'This is better than killing *him*! Now he'll suffer for the rest of his life!'

'God help you, Gail!' Bannon said and snatched the gun from her, hurled it away, face tight with revulsion.

'Ah, *Jesus*!' cried Langford from behind Bannon, pushing him aside, stumbling as he knelt beside the dead horse and cradled its noble-looking head in his lap. 'Aw, Christ . . . ' His voice broke and a tear tracked through the dirt and blood on his face as he rocked back and forth, a beaten man.

'How do *you* like being ruined, you bastard!' Gail screamed, but the smile of triumph froze on her face as she turned to Bannon. 'What's wrong? He deserved this!'

'You deserve each other,' he growled bitterly, wadded his kerchief over his shoulder wound, then turned and walked away. He didn't answer when she called his name, didn't even look back.

We do hope that you have enjoyed reading this large print book.

Did you know that all of our titles are available for purchase?

We publish a wide range of high quality large print books including:
Romances, Mysteries, Classics
General Fiction
Non Fiction and Westerns

Special interest titles available in large print are:
The Little Oxford Dictionary
Music Book, Song Book
Hymn Book, Service Book

Also available from us courtesy of Oxford University Press:
Young Readers' Dictionary
(large print edition)
Young Readers' Thesaurus
(large print edition)

For further information or a free brochure, please contact us at:
Ulverscroft Large Print Books Ltd.,
The Green, Bradgate Road, Anstey,
Leicester, LE7 7FU, England.
Tel: (00 44) **0116 236 4325**
Fax: (00 44) **0116 234 0205**

THE BOUNTYMEN

Tom Anson

Tom Quinlan headed a bunch of other bounty hunters to bring in the long-sought Dave Cull, who was not expected to be alone. That they would face difficulties was clear, but an added complication was the attitude of Quinlan's strong-minded woman, Belle. And suddenly, mixed up in the search for Cull, was the dangerous Arn Lazarus and his men. Hunters and hunted were soon embroiled in a deadly game whose outcome none could predict.

THE EARLY LYNCHING

Mark Bannerman

Young Rice Sheridan leaves behind his adoptive Comanche parents and finds work on the Double Star Ranch. Three years later, he and his boss, Seth Early, are ambushed by outlaws, and their leader, the formidable Vince Corby, brutally murders Early. Rice survives and reaches town. Pitched into a maelstrom of deception and treachery, Rice is nevertheless determined that nothing will prevent him from taking revenge on Corby. But he faces death at every turn . . .

RENEGADE BLOOD

Johnny Mack Bride

Joe Gage was a drifter who'd never had a regular job until, in Dearman, Colorado, he found steady work and met a pretty girl. But he also fell foul of the feared Hunsen clan, a family of mad, murderous renegades who decided he was their enemy. Joe had two choices: give up his future and ride out of the territory, or fight against the 'Family from Hell'. He made his decision, but he was just one man against many.

RIO REPRISAL

Jake Douglas

Life had taken on a new meaning for Jordan and all he wanted was to be left alone, but it was not to be. Back home, there were only blackened ruins and Mandy had been taken by the feared Apache, Wolf Taker. The only men Jordan could turn to for help were the outlaws with whom he had once ridden, but their price was high and bloody. Nevertheless, Jordan was prepared to tear the entire southwest apart as long as he found Mandy.

DEATH MARCH IN MONTANA

Bill Foord

Held under armed guard in a Union prison camp, Captain Pat Quaid learns that the beautiful wife of the sadistic commandant wants her husband killed. She engineers the escape of Quaid and his young friend Billy Childs in exchange for Quaid's promise to turn hired gunman. He has reasons enough to carry out the promise, but he's never shot a man in cold blood. Can he do it for revenge, hatred or love?

A LAND TO DIE FOR

Tyler Hatch

There were two big ranches in the valley: Box T and Flag. Ben Tanner's Box T was the larger and he ran things his way. Wes Flag seemed content to play second fiddle to Tanner — until he married Shirley. But the trouble hit the valley and soon everyone was involved. Now it was all down to Tanner's loyal ramrod, Jesse McCord. He had to face some tough decisions if he was to bring peace to the troubled range — and come out alive.